SAMANTHA ON THE WOMAN QUESTION

BY

MARIETTA HOLLEY

Samantha On The Woman Question

I

"SHE WANTED HER RIGHTS"

Lorinda Cagwin invited Josiah and me to a reunion of the Allen family at her home nigh Washington, D.C., the birthplace of the first Allen we knowed anything about, and Josiah said:

"Bein' one of the best lookin' and influential Allens on earth now, it would be expected on him to attend to it."

And I fell in with the idee, partly to be done as I would be done by if it wuz the relation on my side, and partly because by goin' I could hit two birds with one stun, as the poet sez. Indeed, I could hit four on 'em.

My own cousin, Diantha Trimble, lived in a city nigh Lorinda's and I had promised to visit her if I wuz ever nigh her, and help bear her burdens for a spell, of which burden more anon and bom-by.

Diantha wuz one bird, the Reunion another, and the third bird I had in my mind's eye wuz the big outdoor meeting of the suffragists that wuz to be held in the city where Diantha lived, only a little ways from Lorinda's.

And the fourth bird and the biggest one I wuz aimin' to hit from this tower of ourn wuz Washington, D.C. I wanted to visit the Capitol of our country, the center of our great civilization that stands like the sun in the solar system, sendin' out beams of power and wisdom and law and order, and justice and injustice, and money and oratory, and talk and talk, and wind and everything, to the uttermost points of our vast possessions, and from them clear to the ends of the earth. I wanted to see it, I wanted to like a dog. So we laid out to go.

Lorinda lived on the old Allen place, and I always sot store by her, and her girl, Polly, wuz, as Thomas J. said, a peach. She had spent one of her college vacations with us, and a sweeter, prettier, brighter girl I don't want to see. Her name is Pauline, but everybody calls her Polly.

The Cagwins are rich, and Polly had every advantage money could give, and old Mom Nater gin her a lot of advantages money couldn't buy, beauty and intellect, a big generous heart and charm. And you know the Cagwins couldn't bought that at no price. Charm in a girl is like the perfume in a rose, and can't be bought or sold. And you can't handle or describe either on 'em exactly. But what a influence they have; how they lay holt of your heart and fancy.

Royal Gray, the young man who wuz payin' attention to her, stopped once for a day or two in Jonesville with Polly and her Ma on their way to the Cagwins' camp in the

Adirondacks. And we all liked him so well that we agreed in givin' him this extraordinary praise, we said he wuz worthy of Polly, we knowed of course that wuz the highest enconium possible for us to give.

Good lookin', smart as a whip, and deep, you could see that by lookin' into his eyes, half laughin' and half serious eyes and kinder sad lookin' too under the fun, as eyes must be in this world of ourn if they look back fur, or ahead much of any. A queer world this is, and kinder sad and mysterious, behind all the good and glory on't.

He wuz jest out of Harvard school and as full of life and sperits as a colt let loose in a clover field. He went out in the hay field, he and Polly, and rode home on top of a load of hay jest as nateral and easy and bare-headed as if he wuz workin' for wages, and he the only son of a millionaire — we all took to him.

Well, when the news got out that I wuz goin' to visit Washington, D.C., all the neighbors wanted to send errents by me. Betsy Bobbet Slimpsey wanted a dozen Patent Office books for scrap books for her poetry.

Uncle Nate Gowdey wanted me to go to the Agricultural Buro and git him a paper of lettuce seed. And Solomon Sypher wanted me to git him a new kind of string beans and some cowcumber seeds.

Uncle Jarvis Bentley, who wuz goin' to paint his house, wanted me to ask the President what kind of paint he used on the White House. He thought it ort to be a extra kind to stand the sharp glare that wuz beatin' down on it constant, and to ask him if he didn't think the paint would last longer and the glare be mollified some if they used pure white and clear ile in it, and left off whitewash and karseen.

Ardelia Rumsey, who is goin' to be married, wanted me, if I see any new kinds of bedquilt patterns at the White House or the Senator's housen, to git patterns for 'em. She said she wuz sick of sun flowers and blazin' stars. She thought mebby they'd have sunthin' new, spread eagle style. She said her feller wuz goin' to be connected with the Govermunt and she thought it would be appropriate.

And I asked her how. And she said he wuz goin' to git a patent on a new kind of jack knife.

I told her that if she wanted a govermunt quilt and wanted it appropriate she ort to have a crazy quilt.

And she said she had jest finished a crazy quilt with seven thousand pieces of silk in it, and each piece trimmed with seven hundred stitches of feather stitchin' — she'd counted 'em. And then I remembered seein' it. There wuz a petition fer wimmen's rights and I remember Ardelia couldn't sign it for lack of time. She wanted to, but she hadn't got the quilt more than half done. It took the biggest heft of two years to do it. And so less important things had to be put aside.

And Ardelia's mother wanted to sign it, but she couldn't owin' to a bed-spread she wuz makin'. She wuz quiltin' in Noah's Ark and all the animals on a Turkey red quilt. I remember she wuz quiltin' the camel that day and couldn't be disturbed, so we didn't git the names. It took the old lady three years, and when it wuz done it wuz a sight to behold, though I wouldn't want to sleep under so many animals. But folks went from fur and near to see it, and I enjoyed lookin' at it that day.

Zebulin Coon wanted me to carry a new hen coop of hisen to git patented.

And I thought to myself I wonder if they will ask me to carry a cow.

And sure enough Elnathan Purdy wanted me to dicker for a calf from Mount

Vernon, swop one of his yearlin's for it.

But the errents Serepta Pester sent wuz fur more hefty and momentous than all the rest put together, calves, hen coop, cow and all.

And when she told 'em over to me, and I meditated on her reasons for sendin' 'em and her need of havin' 'em done, I felt that I would do the errents for her if a breath wuz left in my body. She come for a all day's visit; and though she is a vegetable widow and humbly, I wuz middlin' glad to see her. But thinkses I as I carried her things into my bedroom, "She'll want to send some errent by me"; and I wondered what it would be.

And so it didn't surprise me when she asked me if I would lobby a little for her in Washington. I spozed it wuz some new kind of tattin' or fancy work. I told her I shouldn't have much time but would try to git her some if I could.

And she said she wanted me to lobby myself. And then I thought mebby it wuz a new kind of dance and told her, "I wuz too old to lobby, I hadn't lobbied a step since I wuz married."

And then she explained she wanted me to canvas some of the Senators.

And I hung back and asked her in a cautious tone, "How many she wanted canvassed, and how much canvas it would take?"

I had a good many things to buy for my tower, and though I wanted to obleege Serepta, I didn't feel like runnin' into any great expense for canvas.

And then she broke off from that subject, and said she wanted her rights and wanted the Whiskey Ring broke up.

And she talked a sight about her children, and how bad she felt to be parted from 'em, and how she used to worship her husband and how her hull life wuz ruined and the Whiskey Ring had done it, that and wimmen's helpless condition under the law and she cried and wep' and I did. And right while I wuz cryin' onto that gingham apron, she made me promise to carry them two errents of hern to the President and git 'em done for her if I possibly could.

She wanted the Whiskey Ring destroyed and her rights, and she wanted 'em both inside of two weeks.

I told her I didn't believe she could git 'em done inside that length of time, but I would tell the President about it, and I thought more'n likely as not he would want to do right by her. "And," sez I, "if he sets out to, he can haul them babies of yourn out of that Ring pretty sudden."

And then to git her mind offen her sufferin's, I asked how her sister Azuba wuz gittin' along? I hadn't heard from her for years. She married Phileman Clapsaddle, and Serepty spoke out as bitter as a bitter walnut, and sez she:

"She's in the poor-house."

"Why, Serepta Pester!" sez I, "what do you mean?"

"I mean what I say, my sister, Azuba Clapsaddle, is in the poor-house."

"Why, where is their property gone?" sez I. "They wuz well off. Azuba had five thousand dollars of her own when she married him."

"I know it," sez she, "and I can tell you, Josiah Alien's wife, where their property has gone, it has gone down Phileman Clapsaddle's throat. Look down that man's throat and you will see 150 acres of land, a good house and barn, twenty sheep and forty head of cattle."

"Why-ee!" sez I.

"Yes, and you'll see four mules, a span of horses, two buggies, a double sleigh, and three buffalo robes. He's drinked 'em all up, and two horse rakes, a cultivator, and a thrashin' machine."

"Why-ee!" sez I agin. "And where are the children?"

"The boys have inherited their father's habits and drink as bad as he duz and the oldest girl has gone to the bad."

"Oh dear! oh dear me!" sez I, and we both sot silent for a spell. And then thinkin' I must say sunthin' and wantin' to strike a safe subject and a good lookin' one, I sez:

"Where is your Aunt Cassandra's girl? That pretty girl I see to your house once?"

"That girl is in the lunatick asylum."

"Serepta Pester," sez I, "be you tellin' the truth?"

"Yes, I be, the livin' truth. She went to New York to buy millinery goods for her mother's store. It wuz quite cool when she left home and she hadn't took off her winter clothes, and it come on brilin' hot in the city, and in goin' about from store to store the heat and hard work overcome her and she fell down in a sort of faintin' fit and wuz called drunk and dragged off to a police court by a man who wuz a animal in human shape. And he misused her in such a way that she never got over the horror of what befell her when she come to to find herself at the mercy of a brute in a man's shape. She went into a melancholy madness and wuz sent to the asylum."

I sithed a long and mournful sithe and sot silent agin for quite a spell.

But thinkin' I must be sociable I sez:

"Your aunt Cassandra is well, I spoze?"

"She is moulderin' in jail," sez she.

"In jail? Cassandra in jail!"

"Yes, in jail." And Serepta's tone wuz now like worm-wood and gall.

"You know she owns a big property in tenement houses and other buildings where she lives. Of course her taxes wuz awful high, and she didn't expect to have any voice in tellin' how that money, a part of her own property that she earned herself in a store, should be used. But she had been taxed high for new sidewalks in front of some of her buildin's. And then another man come into power in that ward, and he naterally wanted to make some money out of her, so he ordered her to build new sidewalks. And she wouldn't tear up a good sidewalk to please him or anybody else, so she wuz put to jail for refusin' to comply with the law."

Thinkses I, I don't believe the law would have been so hard on her if she hadn't been so humbly. The Pesters are a humbly lot. But I didn't think it out loud, and didn't ophold the law for feelin' so. I sez in pityin' tones, for I wuz truly sorry for Cassandra Keeler:

"How did it end?"

"It hain't ended," sez she, "it only took place a month ago and she has got her grit up and won't pay; and no knowin' how it will end; she lays there amoulderin'."

I don't believe Cassanda wuz mouldy, but that is Serepta's way of talkin', very flowery.

"Well," sez I, "do you think the weather is goin' to moderate?"

I truly felt that I dassent speak to her about any human bein' under the sun, not knowin' what turn she would give to the talk, bein' so embittered. But I felt that the weather wuz safe, and cotton stockin's, and hens, and factory cloth, and I kep' her down on them for more'n two hours.

But good land! I can't blame her for bein' embittered agin men and the laws they've made, for it seems as if I never see a human creeter so afflicted as Serepta Pester has been all her life.

Why, her sufferin's date back before she wuz born, and that's goin' pretty fur back. Her father and mother had some difficulty and he wuz took down with billerous colick, voylent four weeks before Serepta wuz born. And some think it wuz the hardness between 'em and some think it wuz the gripin' of the colick when he made his will, anyway he willed Serepta away, boy or girl whichever it wuz, to his brother up on the Canada line.

So when Serepta wuz born (and born a girl ontirely onbeknown to her) she wuz took right away from her mother and gin to this brother. Her mother couldn't help herself, he had the law on his side. But it killed her. She drooped away and died before the baby wuz a year old. She wuz a affectionate, tenderhearted woman and her husband wuz overbearin' and stern always.

But it wuz this last move of hisen that killed her, for it is pretty tough on a mother to have her baby, a part of her own life, took right out of her own arms and gin to a stranger. For this uncle of hern wuz a entire stranger to Serepta, and almost like a stranger to her father, for he hadn't seen him since he wuz a boy, but knew he hadn't any children and spozed that he wuz rich and respectable. But the truth wuz he had been runnin' down every way, had lost his property and his character, wuz dissipated and mean. But the will wuz made and the law stood. Men are ashamed now to think that the law wuz ever in voge, but it wuz, and is now in some of the states, and the poor young mother couldn't help herself. It has always been the boast of our American law that it takes care of wimmen. It took care of her. It held her in its strong protectin' grasp so tight that the only way she could slip out of it wuz to drop into the grave, which she did in a few months. Then it leggo.

But it kep' holt of Serepta, it bound her tight to her uncle while he run through with what property she had, while he sunk lower and lower until at last he needed the very necessaries of life and then he bound her out to work to a woman who kep' a drinkin' den and the lowest hant of vice.

Twice Serepta run away, bein' virtuous but humbly, but them strong protectin' arms of the law that had held her mother so tight reached out and dragged her back agin. Upheld by them her uncle could compel her to give her service wherever he wanted her to work, and he wuz owin' this woman and she wanted Serepta's work, so she had to submit.

But the third time she made a effort so voylent that she got away. A good woman, who bein' nothin' but a woman couldn't do anything towards onclinchin' them powerful arms that wuz protectin' her, helped her to slip through 'em. And Serepta come to Jonesville to live with a sister of that good woman; changed her name so's it wouldn't be so easy to find her; grew up to be a nice industrious girl. And when the woman she wuz took by died she left Serepta quite a handsome property.

And finally she married Lank Burpee, and did considerable well it wuz spozed. Her property, put with what little he had, made 'em a comfortable home and they had two pretty children, a boy and a girl. But when the little girl wuz a baby he took to drinkin', neglected his bizness, got mixed up with a whiskey ring, whipped Serepta—not so very hard. He went accordin' to law, and the law of the United States don't approve of a man's whippin' his wife enough to endanger her life, it sez it don't. He made every move of hisen lawful and felt that Serepta hadn't ort to complain and feel hurt. But a good whippin' will make anybody feel hurt, law or no law. And then he parted with her and got her property and her two little children. Why, it seemed as if everything under the sun and moon, that could happen to a woman, had happened to Serepta, painful things and gauldin'.

Jest before Lank parted with her, she fell on a broken sidewalk: some think he tripped her up, but it never wuz proved. But anyway Serepta fell and broke her hip hone; and her husband sued the corporation and got ten thousand dollars for it. Of course the law give the money to him and she never got a cent of it. But she wouldn't have made any fuss over that, knowin' that the law of the United States wuz such. But what made it so awful mortifyin' to her wuz, that while she wuz layin' there achin' in splints, he took that very money and used it to court up another woman with. Gin her presents, jewelry, bunnets, head-dresses, artificial flowers out of Serepta's own hip money.

And I don't know as anything could be much more gauldin' to a woman than that— while she lay there groanin' in splints, to have her husband take the money for her own broken bones and dress up another woman like a doll with it.

But the law gin it to him, and he wuz only availin' himself of the glorious liberty of our free Republic, and doin' as he wuz a mind to. And it wuz spozed that that very hip money wuz what made the match. For before she wuz fairly out of splints he got a divorce from her and married agin. And by the help of Serepta's hip money and the Whiskey Ring he got her two little children away from her.

II

"THEY CAN'T BLAME HER"

And I wonder if there is a woman in the land that can blame Serepta for gittin' mad and wantin' her rights and wantin' the Whiskey Ring broke up, when they think how she's been fooled round with by men; willed away, and whipped, and parted with, and stole from. Why, they can't blame her for feelin' fairly savage about 'em, as she duz.

For as she sez to me once, when we wuz talkin' it over, how everything had happened to her. "Yes," sez she, with a axent like bone-set and vinegar, "and what few things hain't happened to me has happened to my folks."

And sure enough I couldn't dispute her. Trouble and wrongs and sufferin's seemed to be epidemic in the race of Pester wimmen. Why, one of her aunts on her father's side, Huldah Pester, married for her first husband, Eliphelet Perkins. He wuz a minister, rode on a circuit, and he took Huldah on it too, and she rode round with him on it a good deal of the time. But she never loved to, she wuz a woman that loved to be still, and kinder settled down at home.

But she loved Eliphelet so well that she would do anything to please him, so she rode round with him on that circuit till she wuz perfectly fagged out.

He wuz a dretful good man to her, but he wuz kinder poor and they had hard times to git along. But what property they had wuzn't taxed, so that helped some, and Huldah would make one dollar go a good ways.

No, their property wuzn't taxed till Eliphelet died. Then the supervisor taxed it the very minute the breath left his body; run his horse, so it wuz said, so's to be sure to git it onto the tax list, and comply with the law.

You see Eliphelet's salary stopped when his breath did. And I spoze the law thought, seein' she wuz havin' trouble, she might jest as well have a little more; so it taxed all the property it never had taxed a cent for before.

But she had this to console her that the law didn't forgit her in her widowhood. No; the law is quite thoughtful of wimmen by spells. It sez it protects wimmen. And I spoze that in some mysterious way, too deep for wimmen to understand, it wuz protectin' her now.

Well, she suffered along and finally married agin. I wondered why she did. But she wuz such a quiet, home-lovin' woman that it wuz spozed she wanted to settle down and be kinder still and sot. But of all the bad luck she had. She married on short acquaintance, and he proved to be a perfect wanderer. He couldn't keep still, it wuz spozed to be a mark.

He moved Huldah thirteen times in two years, and at last he took her into a cart, a sort of covered wagon, and traveled right through the western states with her. He wanted to see the country and loved to live in the wagon, it wuz his make. And, of course, the law give him control of her body, and she had to go where he moved it, or else part with him. And I spoze the law thought it wuz guardin' and nourishin' her when it wuz joltin' her over them prairies and mountains and abysses. But it jest kep' her shook up the hull of the time.

It wuz the regular Pester luck.

And then another of her aunts, Drusilly Pester, married a industrious, hard-workin' man, one that never drinked, wuz sound on the doctrines, and give good measure to his customers, he wuz a groceryman. And a master hand for wantin' to foller the laws of his country as tight as laws could be follered. And so knowin' that the law approved of moderate correction for wimmen, and that "a man might whip his wife, but not enough to endanger her life"; he bein' such a master hand for wantin' to do everything faithful and do his very best for his customers, it wuz spozed he wanted to do the best for the law, and so when he got to whippin' Drusilly, he would whip her too severe, he would be too faithful to it.

You see what made him whip her at all wuz she wuz cross to him. They had nine little children, she thought two or three children would be about all one woman could bring up well by hand, when that hand wuz so stiff and sore with hard work.

But he had read some scareful talk from high quarters about Race Suicide. Some men do git real wrought up about it and want everybody to have all the children they can, jest as fast as they can, though wimmen don't all feel so.

Aunt Hetty Sidman said, "If men had to born 'em and nuss 'em themselves, she didn't spoze they would be so enthusiastick about it after they had had a few, 'specially if they done their own housework themselves," and Aunt Hetty said that some of the men who wuz exhortin' wimmen to have big families, had better spend some of their strength and wind in tryin' to make this world a safer place for children to be born into.

She said they'd be better off in Nonentity than here in this world with saloons on every corner, and war-dogs howlin' at 'em.

I don't know exactly what she meant by Nonentity, but guess she meant the world we all stay in, before we are born into this one.

Aunt Hetty has lost five boys, two by battle and three by licensed saloons, that makes her talk real bitter, but to resoom. I told Josiah that men needn't worry about Race Suicide, for you might as well try to stop a hen from makin' a nest, as to stop wimmen from wantin' a baby to love and hold on her heart. But sez I, "Folks ort to be moderate and mejum in babies as well as in everything else."

But Drusilly's husband wanted twelve boys he said, to be law-abidin' citizens as their Pa wuz, and a protection to the Govermunt, and to be ready to man the new warships, if a war broke out. But her babies wuz real pretty and cunning, and she wuz so weak-minded she couldn't enjoy the thought that if our male statesmen got to scrappin' with some other nation's male law-makers and made another war, of havin' her grown-up babies face the cannons. I spoze it wuz when she wuz so awful tired she felt so.

You see she had to do every mite of her housework, and milk cows, and make butter and cheese, and cook and wash and scour, and take all the care of the children day and night in sickness and health, and make their clothes and keep 'em clean. And when there wuz so many of 'em and she enjoyin' real poor health, I spoze she sometimes thought more of her own achin' back than she did of the good of the Govermunt—and she would git kinder discouraged sometimes and be cross to him. And knowin' his own motives wuz so high and loyal, he felt that he ort to whip her, so he did.

And what shows that Drusilly wuzn't so bad after all and did have her good streaks and a deep reverence for the law is, that she stood his whippin's first-rate, and never whipped him. Now she wuz fur bigger than he wuz, weighed eighty pounds the most, and might have whipped him if the law had been such. But they wuz both law-abidin' and wanted to keep every preamble, so she stood it to be whipped, and never once whipped him in all the seventeen years they lived together. She died when her twelfth child wuz born. There wuz jest ten months difference between that and the one next older. And they said she often spoke out in her last sickness, and said, "Thank fortune, I've always kep' the law!" And they said the same thought wuz a great comfort to him in his last moments. He died about a year after she did, leavin' his second wife with twins and a good property.

Then there wuz Abagail Pester. She married a sort of a high-headed man, though one that paid his debts, wuz truthful, good lookin', and played well on the fiddle. Why, it seemed as if he had almost every qualification for makin' a woman happy, only he had this one little eccentricity, he would lock up Abagail's clothes every time he got mad at her.

Of course the law give her clothes to him, and knowin' that it wuz the law in the state where they lived, she wouldn't have complained only when they had company. But it wuz mortifyin', nobody could dispute it, to have company come and have nothin' to put on. Several times she had to withdraw into the woodhouse, and stay most all day there shiverin', and under the suller stairs and round in clothes presses. But he boasted in prayer meetin's and on boxes before grocery stores that he wuz a law-abidin' citizen, and he wuz. Eben Flanders wouldn't lie for anybody.

But I'll bet Abagail Flanders beat our old revolutionary four-mothers in thinkin' out new laws, when she lay round under stairs and behind barrels in her night-gown. When a man hides his wife's stockin's and petticoats it is governin' without the consent of the governed. If you don't believe it you'd ort to peeked round them barrels and seen Abagail's eyes, they had hull reams of by-laws in 'em and preambles, and Declarations of Independence, so I've been told. But it beat everything I ever hearn on, the lawful sufferin's of them wimmen. For there wuzn't nothin' illegal about one single trouble of theirn. They suffered accordin' to law, every one on 'em. But it wuz tuff for 'em, very tuff. And their bein' so dretful humbly wuz another drawback to 'em, though that too wuz perfectly lawful, as everybody knows.

And Serepta looked as bad agin as she would otherwise on account of her teeth. It wuz after Lank had begun to git after this other woman, and wuz indifferent to his wife's looks that Serepta had a new set of teeth on her upper jaw. And they sot out and made her look so bad it fairly made her ache to look at herself in the glass. And they hurt her gooms too, and she carried 'em back to the dentist and wanted him to make her another set, but he acted mean and wouldn't take 'em back, and sued Lank for the pay. And they had a law-suit. And the law bein' such that a woman can't testify in court, in any matter that is of mutual interest to husband and wife, and Lank wantin' to act mean, said that they wuz good sound teeth.

And there Serepta sot right in front of 'em with her gooms achin' and her face all swelled out, and lookin' like furiation, and couldn't say a word. But she had to give in to the law. And ruther than go toothless she wears 'em to this day, and I believe it is the raspin' of them teeth aginst her gooms and her discouraged, mad feelin's every time she looks in the glass that helps embitter her towards men, and the laws men have made, so's a woman can't have control of her own teeth and her own bones.

Serepta went home about 5 P.M., I promisin' sacred to do her errents for her.

And I gin a deep, happy sithe after I shot the door behind her, and I sez to Josiah I do hope that's the very last errent we will have to carry to Washington, D.C., for the Jonesvillians.

"Yes," says he, "an' I guess I will get a fresh pail of water and hang on the tea kettle for you."

"And," I says, "it's pretty early for supper, but I'll start it, for I do feel kinder gone to the stomach. Sympathy is real exhaustin'. Sometimes I think it tires me more'n hard work. And Heaven knows I sympathized with Serepta. I felt for her full as much as if she was one of the relations on his side."

But if you'll believe it, I had hardly got the words out of my mouth and Josiah had jest laid holt of the water pail, when in comes Philander Dagget, the President of the

Jonesville Creation Searchin' Society and, of course, he had a job for us to do on our tower. This Society was started by the leadin' men of Jonesville, for the purpose of searchin' out and criticizin' the affairs of the world, an' so far as possible advisin' and correctin' the meanderin's an' wrong-doin's of the universe.

This Society, which we call the C.S.S. for short, has been ruther quiet for years. But sence woman's suffrage has got to be such a prominent question, they bein' so bitterly opposed to it, have reorganized and meet every once in a while, to sneer at the suffragettes and poke fun at 'em and show in every way they can their bitter antipathy to the cause.

Philander told me if I see anything new and strikin' in the way of Society badges and regalia, to let him know about it, for he said the C.S.S. was goin' to take a decided stand and show their colors. They wuz goin' to help protect his women endangered sect, an' he wanted sunthin' showy and suggestive.

I thought of a number of badges and mottoes that I felt would be suitable for this Society, but dassent tell 'em to him, for his idees and mine on this subject are as fur apart as the two poles. He talked awful bitter to me once about it, and I sez to him:

"Philander, the world is full of good men, and there are also bad men in the world, and, sez I, did you ever in your born days see a bad man that wuzn't opposed to Woman's Suffrage? All the men who trade in, and profit by, the weakness and sin of men and women, they every one of 'em, to a man, fight agin it. And would they do this if they didn't think that their vile trades would suffer if women had the right to vote? It is the great-hearted, generous, noble man who wants women to become a real citizen with himself—which she is not now—she is only a citizen just enough to be taxed equally with man, or more exhorbitantly, and be punished and executed by the law she has no hand in makin'."

Philander sed, "I have always found it don't pay to talk with women on matters they don't understand."

An' he got up and started for the door, an' Josiah sed, "No, it don't pay, not a cent; I've always said so."

But I told Philander I'd let him know if I see anything appropriate to the C.S.S. Holdin' back with a almost Herculaneum effort the mottoes and badges that run through my mind as bein' appropriate to their society; knowin' it would make him so mad if I told him of 'em—he never would neighbor with us again. And in three days' time we sot sail. We got to the depo about an hour too early, but I wuz glad we wuz on time, for it would have worked Josiah up dretfully ef we hadn't been, for he had spent most of the latter part of the night in gittin' up and walkin' out to the clock seein' if it wuz train time. Jest before we started, who should come runnin' down to the depo but Sam Nugent wantin' to send a errent by me to Washington. He wunk me out to one side of the waitin' room, and ast "if I'd try to git him a license to steal horses."

It kinder runs in the blood of the Nugents to love to steal, and he owned up it did, but he said he wanted the profit of it. But I told him I wouldn't do any sech thing, an' I looked at him in such a witherin' way that I should most probable withered him, only he is blind in one side, and I wuz on the blind side, but he argued with me, and said that it wuz no worse than to give licenses for other kinds of meanness.

He said they give licenses now to steal—steal folkses senses away, and then they could steal everything else, and murder and tear round into every kind of wickedness. But he didn't ask that. He wanted things done fair and square: he jest wanted to steal horses. He wuz goin' West, and he thought he could do a good bizness, and lay up somethin'. If he had a license he shouldn't be afraid of bein' shet up or shot.

But I refused the job with scorn; and jest as I wuz refusin', the cars snorted, and I wuz glad they did. They seemed to express in that wild snort something of the indignation I felt.

The idee!

III

"POLLY'S EYES CROWED TENDER"

Lorinda wuz dretful glad to see us and so wuz her husband and Polly. But

the Reunion had to be put off on account of a spell her husband wuz havin'.

Lorinda said she could not face such a big company as she'd invited while

Hiram wuz havin' a spell, and I agreed with her.

Sez I, "Never, never, would I have invited company whilst Josiah wuz sufferin' with one of his cricks."

Men hain't patient under pain, and outsiders hain't no bizness to hear things they say and tell on 'em. So Polly had to write to the relations puttin' off the Reunion for one week. But Lorinda kep' on cookin' fruit cake and such that would keep, she had plenty of help, but loved to do her company cookin' herself. And seein' the Reunion wuz postponed and Lorinda had time on her hands, I proposed she should go with me to the big out-door meetin' of the Suffragists, which wuz held in a nigh-by city.

"Good land!" sez she, "nothin' would tempt me to patronize anything so brazen and onwomanly as a out-door meetin' of wimmen, and so onhealthy and immodest." I see she looked reproachfully at Polly as she said it. Polly wuz arrangin' some posies in a vase, and looked as sweet as the posies did, but considerable firm too, and I see from Lorinda's looks that Polly wuz one who had to leave father and mother for principle's sake.

But I sez, "You're cookin' this minute, Lorinda, for a out-door meetin'" (she wuz makin' angel cake). "And why is this meetin' any more onwomanly or immodest than the camp-meetin' where you wuz converted, and baptized the next Sunday in the creek?"

"Oh, them wuz religious meetin's," sez she.

"Well," sez I, "mebby these wimmen think their meetin' is religious. You know the Bible sez, 'Faith and works should go together,' and some of the leaders of this movement have showed by their works as religious a sperit and wielded aginst injustice to young workin' wimmen as powerful a weepon as that axe of the 'Postles the Bible tells about. And you said you went every day to the Hudson-Fulton doin's and hearn every out-door lecture; you writ me that there wuz probable a million wimmen attendin' them out-door meetin's, and that wuz curosity and pleasure huntin' that took them, and this is a meetin' of justice and right."

"Oh, shaw!" sez Lorinda agin, with her eye on Polly. "Wimmen have all the rights they want or need." Lorinda's husband bein' rich and lettin' her have her way she is real foot loose, and don't feel the need of any more rights for herself, but I told her then and there some of the wrongs and sufferin's of Serepta Pester, and bein' good-hearted (but obstinate and bigoted) she gin in that the errents wuz hefty, and that Serepta wuz to be pitied, but she insisted that wimmen's votin' wouldn't help matters.

But Euphrasia Pottle, a poor relation from Troy, spoke up. "After my husband died one of my girls went into a factory and gits about half what the men git for the same work, and my oldest girl who teaches in the public school don't git half as much for the same work as men do, and her school rooms are dark, stuffy, onhealthy, and crowded so the children are half-choked for air, and the light so poor they're havin' their eyesight spilte for life, and new school books not needed at all, are demanded constantly, so some-one can make money."

"Yes," sez I, "do you spoze, Lorinda, if intelligent mothers helped control such things they would let their children be made sick and blind and the money that should be used for food for poor hungry children be squandered on on-necessary books they are too faint with hunger to study."

"But wimmen's votin' wouldn't help in such things," sez Lorinda, as she stirred her angel cake vigorously.

But Euphrasia sez, "My niece, Ellen, teaches in a state where wimmen vote and she gits the same wages men git for the same work, and her school rooms are bright and pleasant and sanitary, and the pupils, of course, are well and happy. And if you don't think wimmen can help in such public matters just go to Seattle and see how quick a bad man wuz yanked out of his public office and a good man put in his place, mostly by wimmen's efforts and votes."

"Yes," sez I, "it is a proved fact that wimmen's votes do help in these matters. And do you think, Lorinda, that if educated, motherly, thoughtful wimmen helped make the laws so many little children would be allowed to toil in factories and mines, their tender shoulders bearin' the burden of constant labor that wears out the iron muscles of men?"

Polly's eyes growed tender and wistful, and her little white hands lingered over her posies, and I knowed the hard lot of the poor, the wrongs of wimmen and children, the woes of humanity, wuz pressin' down on her generous young heart. And I could see in her sweet face the brave determination to do and to dare, to try to help ondo the wrongs, and try to lift the burdens from weak and achin' shoulders. But Lorinda kep' on with the same old moth-eaten argument so broke down and feeble it ort to be allowed to die in peace.

"Woman's suffrage would make women neglect their homes and housework and let their children run loose into ruin."

I knowed she said it partly on Polly's account, but I sez in surprise, "Why, Lorinda, it must be you hain't read up on the subject or you would know wherever wimmen has voted they have looked out first of all for the children's welfare. They have raised the age of consent, have closed saloons and other places of licensed evil, and in every way it has been their first care to help 'em to safer and more moral surroundin's, for who has the interest of children more at heart than the mothers who bore them, children who are the light of their eyes and the hope of the future."

Lorinda admitted that the state of the children in the homes of the poor and ignorant wuz pitiful. "But," sez she, "the Bible sez 'ye shall always have the poor with you,' and I spoze we always shall, with all their sufferin's and wants. But," sez she, "in well-to-do homes the children are safe and well off, and don't need any help from woman legislation."

"Why, Lorinda," sez I, "did you ever think on't how such mothers may watch over and be the end of the law to their children with the father's full consent during infancy when they're wrastlin' with teethin', whoopin'-cough, mumps, etc., can be queen of the nursery, dispensor of pure air, sunshine, sanitary, and safe surroundin's in every way, and then in a few years see 'em go from her into dark, overcrowded, unsanitary, carelessly guarded places, to spend the precious hours when they are the most receptive to influence and pass man-made pitfalls on their way to and fro, must stand helpless until in too many cases the innocent healthy child that went from her care returns to her half-blind, a physical and moral wreck. The mother who went down to death's door for 'em, and had most to do in mouldin' their destiny during infancy should have at least equal rights with the father in controllin' their surroundin's during their entire youth, and to do this she must have equal legal power or her best efforts are wasted. That this is just and right is as plain to me as the nose on my face and folks will see it bom-bye and wonder they didn't before.

"And wimmen who suffer most by the lack on't, will be most interested in openin' schools to teach the fine art of domestic service, teachin' young girls how to keep healthy comfortable homes and fit themselves to be capable wives and mothers. I don't say or expect that wimmen's votin' will make black white, or wash all the stains from the legislative body at once, but I say that jest the effort to git wimmen's suffrage has opened hundreds of bolted doors and full suffrage will open hundreds more. And I'm goin' to that woman's suffrage meetin' if I walk afoot."

But here Josiah spoke up, I thought he wuz asleep, he wuz layin' on the lounge with a paper over his face. But truly the word, "Woman's Suffrage," rousts him up as quick as a mouse duz a drowsy cat, so, sez he, "I can't let you go, Samantha, into any such dangerous and onwomanly affair."

"Let?" sez I in a dry voice; "that's a queer word from one old pardner to another."

"I'm responsible for your safety, Samantha, and if anybody goes to that dangerous and onseemly meetin' I will. Mebby Polly would like to go with me." As stated, Polly is as pretty as a pink posy, and no matter how old a man is, nor how interestin' and noble his pardner is, he needs girl blinders, yes, he needs 'em from the cradle to the grave. But few, indeed, are the female pardners who can git him to wear 'em.

He added, "You know I represent you legally, Samantha; what I do is jest the same as though you did it."

Sez I, "Mebby that is law, but whether it is gospel is another question. But if you represent me, Josiah, you will have to carry out my plans; I writ to Diantha Smith Trimble that if I went to the city I'd take care of Aunt Susan a night or two, and rest her a spell; you know Diantha is a widder and too poor to hire a nurse. But seein' you represent me you can set up with her Ma a night or two; she's bed-rid and you'll have to lift her round some, and give her her medicine and take care of Diantha's twins, and let her git a good sleep."

"Well, as it were—Samantha—you know—men hain't expected to represent wimmen in everything, it is mostly votin' and tendin' big meetin's and such."

"Oh, I see," sez I; "men represent wimmen when they want to, and when they don't wimmen have got to represent themselves."

"Well, yes, Samantha, sunthin' like that."

He didn't say anything more about representin' me, and Polly said she wuz goin' to ride in the parade with some other college girls. Lorinda's linement looked dark and forbiddin' as Polly stated in her gentle, but firm way this ultimatum. Lorinda hated the idee of Polly's jinin' in what she called onwomanly and immodest doin's, but I looked beamin'ly at her and gloried in her principles.

After she went out Lorinda said to me in a complainin' way, "I should think that a girl that had every comfort and luxury would be contented and thankful, and be willin' to stay to home and act like a lady."

Sez I, "Nothin' could keep Polly from actin' like a lady, and mebby it is because she is so well off herself that makes her sorry for other young girls that have nothin' but poverty and privation."

"Oh, nonsense!" sez Lorinda. But I knowed jest how it wuz. Polly bein' surrounded by all the good things money could give, and bein' so tender-hearted her heart ached for other young girls, who had to spend the springtime of their lives in the hard work of earnin' bread for themselves and dear ones, and she longed to help 'em to livin' wages, so they could exist without the wages of sin, and too many on 'em had to choose between them black wages and starvation. She wanted to help 'em to better surroundin's and she knowed the best weepon she could put into their hands to fight the wolves of Want and Temptation, wuz the ballot. Polly hain't a mite like her Ma, she favors the Smiths more, her grand-ma on her pa's side wuz a Smith and a woman of brains and principle.

Durin' my conversation with Lorinda, I inquired about Royal Gray, for as stated, he wuz a great favorite of ourn, and I found out (and I could see it gaulded her) that when Polly united with the Suffragists he shied off some, and went to payin' attention to another girl. Whether it wuz to make Polly jealous and bring her round to his way of thinkin', I didn't know, but mistrusted, for I could have took my oath that he loved Polly deeply and truly. To be sure he hadn't confided in me, but there is a language of the eyes, when the soul speaks through 'em, and as I'd seen him look at Polly my own soul had hearn and understood that silent language and translated it, that Polly wuz the light of his eyes, and the one woman in the world for him. And I couldn't think his heart had changed so sudden. But knowin' as I did the elastic nature of manly affection, I felt dubersome.

This other girl, Maud Vincent, always said to her men friends, it wuz onwomanly to try to vote. She wuz one of the girls who always gloried in bein' a runnin' vine when there wuz any masculine trees round to lean on and twine about. One who always jined in with all the idees they promulgated, from neckties to the tariff, who declared cigar smoke wuz so agreeable and welcome; it did really make her deathly sick, but she would choke herself cheerfully and willin'ly if by so chokin' she could gain manly favor and admiration.

She said she didn't believe in helpin' poor girls, they wuz well enough off as it wuz, she wuz sure they didn't feel hunger and cold as rich girls did, their skin wuz thicker and their stomachs different and stronger, and constant labor didn't harm them, and working girls didn't need recreation as rich girls did, and woman's suffrage wouldn't help them any; in her opinion it would harm them, and anyway the poor wuz on-grateful.

She had the usual arguments on the tip of her tongue, for old Miss Vincent, the aunt she lived with, wuz a ardent She Aunty and very prominent in the public meetin's the She Auntys have to try to compel the Suffragists not to have public meetin's. They talk a good deal in public how onwomanly and immodest it is for wimmen to talk in public. And she wuz one of the foremost ones in tryin' to git up a school to teach wimmen civics, to prove that they mustn't ever have anything to do with civics.

Yes, old Miss Vincent wuz a real active, ardent She Aunty, and Maud Genevieve takes after her. Royal Gray, his handsome attractive personality, and his millions, had long been the goal of Maud's ambition. And how ardently did she hail the coolness growing between him and Polly, the little rift in the lute, and how zealously did she labor to make it larger.

Polly and Royal had had many an argument on the subject, that is, he would begin by makin' fun of the Suffragists and their militant doin's, which if he'd thought on't wuz sunthin' like what his old revolutionary forbears went through for the same reasons, bein' taxed without representation, and bein' burdened and punished by the law they had no voice in making, only the Suffragettes are not nearly so severe with their opposers, they haven't drawed any blood yet. Why, them old Patriots we revere so, would consider their efforts for freedom exceedingly gentle and tame compared to their own bloody battles.

And Royal would make light of the efforts of college girls to help workin' girls, and the encouragement and aid they'd gin 'em when they wuz strikin' for less death-dealin' hours of labor, and livin' wages, and so forth. I don't see how such a really noble young man as Royal ever come to argy that way, but spoze it wuz the dead hand of some rough onreasonable old ancestor reachin' up out of the shadows of the past and pushin' him on in the wrong direction.

So when he begun to ridicule what Polly's heart wuz sot on, when she felt that he wuz fightin' agin right and justice, before they knowed it both pairs of bright eyes would git to flashin' out angry sparks, and hash words would be said on both sides. That old long-buried Tory ancestor of hisen eggin' him on, so I spoze, and Polly's generous sperit rebellin' aginst the injustice and selfishness, and mebby some warlike ancestor of hern pushin' her on to say hash things. 'Tennyrate he had grown less attentive to her, and wuz bestowin' his time and attentions elsewhere.

And when she told him she wuz goin' to ride in the automobile parade of the suffragists, but really ridin' she felt towards truth and justice to half the citizens of the U.S., he wuz mad as a wet hen, a male wet hen, and wuz bound she shouldn't go.

Some men, and mebby it is love that makes 'em feel so (they say it is), and mebby it is selfishness (though they won't own up to it), but they want the women they love to belong to them alone, want to rule absolutely over their hearts, their souls, their bodies, and all their thoughts and aims, desires, and fancies. They don't really say they want 'em to wear veils, and be shet in behind lattice-windowed harems, but I believe they would enjoy it.

They want to be foot loose and heart loose themselves, but always after Ulysses is tired of world wandering, he wants to come back and open the barred doors of home with his own private latch-key, and find Penelope knitting stockings for him with her veil on, waitin' for him.

That sperit is I spoze inherited from the days when our ancestor, the Cave man, would knock down the woman he fancied, with a club, and carry her off into his cave and keep her there shet up. But little by little men are forgettin' their ancestral traits, and men and wimmen are gradually comin' out of their dark caverns into the sunshine (for women too have inherited queer traits and disagreeable ones, but that is another story).

Well, as I said, Royal wuz mad and told Polly that he guessed that the day of the Parade he would take Maud Vincent out in the country in his motor, to gather May-flowers. Polly told him she hoped they would have a good time, and then, after he had gone, drivin' his car lickety-split, harem skarum, owin' to his madness I spoze, Polly went upstairs and cried, for I hearn her, her room wuz next to ourn.

And I deeply respected her for her principles, for he had asked her first to go May-flowering with him the day of the Suffrage meeting. But she refused, havin' in her mind, I spoze, the girls that couldn't hunt flowers, but had to handle weeds and thistles with bare hands (metaforically) and wanted to help them and all workin' wimmen to happier and more prosperous lives.

IV

"STRIVIN' WITH THE EMISSARY"

But I am hitchin' the horse behind the wagon and to resoom backwards. The Reunion wuz put off a week and the Suffrage Meetin' wuz two days away, so I told Lorinda I didn't believe I would have a better time to carry Serepta Pester's errents to Washington, D.C. Josiah said he guessed he would stay and help wait on Hiram Cagwin, and I approved on't, for Lorinda wuz gittin' wore out.

And then Josiah made so light of them errents I felt that he would be a drawback instead of a help, for how could I keep a calm and noble frame of mind befittin' them lofty errents, and how could I carry 'em stiddy with a pardner by my side pokin' fun at 'em, and at me for carryin' 'em, jarrin' my sperit with his scorfin' and onbelievin' talk?

And as I sot off alone in the trolley I thought of how they must have felt in old times a-carryin' the Urim and Thumim. And though I hadn't no idee what them wuz, yet I always felt that the carriers of 'em must have felt solemn and high-strung. Yes, my feelin's wuz such as I felt of the heft and importance of them errents not alone to Serepta Pester, but to the hull race of wimmen that it kep' my mental head rained up so high that I couldn't half see and enjoy the sight of the most beautiful city in the world, and still I spoze its grandeur and glory sort o' filtered down through my conscientiousness, as cloth grows white under the sun's rays onbeknown to it.

Anon I left the trolley and walked some ways afoot. It wuz a lovely day, the sun shone down in golden splendor upon the splendor beneath it. Broad, beautiful clean streets, little fresh green parks, everywhere you could turn about, and big ones full of flowers and fountains, and trees and statutes.

And anon or oftener I passed noble big stun buildings, where everything is made for the nation's good and profit. Money and fish and wisdom and all sorts of patented things and garden seeds and tariffs and resolutions and treaties and laws of every shape and size, good ones and queer ones and reputations and rates and rebates, etc., etc. But it would devour too much time to even name over all that is made and onmade there, even if I knowed by name the innumerable things that are flowin' constant out of that great reservoir of the Nation, with its vast crowd of law-makers settin' on the lid, regulatin' its flow and spreadin' it abroad over the country, thick and thin.

But on I went past the Capitol, the handsomest buildin' on the Globe, standin' in its own Eden of beauty. By the Public Library as long as from our house to Grout Hozleton's, and I guess longer, and every foot on't more beautifler ornamented than tongue can tell. But I didn't dally tryin' to pace off the size on't, though it wuz enormous, for the thought of what I wuz carryin' bore me on almost regardless of my matchless surroundin's and the twinges of rumatiz.

And anon I arrived at the White House, where my hopes and the hopes of my sect and Serepta Pester wuz sot. I will pass over my efforts to git into the Presence, merely sayin' that they were arjous and extreme, and I wouldn't probably have got in at all had not the Presence appeared with a hat on jest goin' out for a walk, and see me as I wuz strivin' with the emissary for entrance. I spoze my noble mean, made more noble fur by the magnitude of what I wuz carryin', impressed him, for suffice it to say inside of five minutes the Presence wuz back in his augience room, and I wuz layin' out them errents of Serepta's in front of him.

He wuz very hefty, a good-lookin' smilin' man, a politer demeanored gentlemanly appearner man I don't want to see. But his linement which had looked so pleasant and cheerful growed gloomy and deprested as I spread them errents before him and sez in conclusion:

"Serepta Pester sent these errents to you, she wanted intemperance done away with, the Whiskey Ring broke up and destroyed, she wanted you to have nothin' stronger than root beer when you had company to dinner, she offerin' to send you some burdock and dandeline roots and some emptins to start it with, and she wanted her rights, and wanted 'em all by week after next without fail."

He sithed hard, and I never see a linement fall furder than hisen fell, and kep' a-fallin'. I pitied him, I see it wuz a hard stent for him to do it in the time she had sot, and he so fleshy too. But knowin' how much wuz at the stake, and how the fate of Serepta and wimmen wuz tremblin' in the balances, I spread them errents out before him. And bein' truthful and above board, I told him that Serepta wuz middlin' disagreeable and very humbly, but she needed her rights jest as much as though she wuz a wax-doll. And I went on and told him how she and her relations had suffered from want of rights, and how dretfully she had suffered from the Ring till I declare talkin' about them little children of hern, and her agony, I got about as fierce actin' as Serepta herself, and entirely onbeknown to myself I talked powerful on intemperance and Rings, and such.

When I got down agin onto my feet I see he had a still more worried and anxious look on his good-natured face, and he sez: "The laws of the United States are such that I can't do them errands, I can't interfere."

"Then," sez I, "why don't you make the United States do right?"

He said sunthin' about the might of the majority, and the powerful corporations and rings, and that sot me off agin. And I talked very powerful and allegored about allowin' a ring to be put round the United States and let a lot of whiskey dealers and corporations lead her round, a pitiful sight for men and angels. Sez I, "How duz it look before the nations to see Columbia led round half-tipsy by a Ring?"

He seemed to think it looked bad, I knew by his looks.

Sez I, "Intemperance is bad for Serepta and bad for the Nation."

He murmured sunthin' about the revenue the liquor trade brought the

Govermunt.

But I sez, "Every penny is money right out of the people's pockets; every dollar the people pay into the liquor traffic that gives a few cents into the treasury, is costin' the people ten times that dollar in the loss intemperance entails, loss of labor, by the inability of drunken men to do anything but wobble and stagger, loss of wealth by the enormous losses of property and taxation, of alms-houses, mad-houses, jails, police forces, paupers' coffins, and the diggin' of thousands and thousands of graves that are filled yearly by them that reel into 'em." Sez I, "Wouldn't it be better for the people to pay that dollar in the first place into the treasury than to let it filter through the dram-seller's hands, a few cents of it fallin' into the national purse at last, putrid and heavy with all these losses and curses and crimes and shames and despairs and agonies?"

He seemed to think it would, I see by the looks of his linement he did. Every honorable man feels so in his heart, and yet they let the Liquor Ring control 'em and lead 'em round. "It is queer, queer as a dog." Sez I, "The intellectual and moral power of the United States are rolled up and thrust into that Whiskey Ring and bein' drove by the whiskey dealers jest where they want to drive 'em." Sez I, "It controls New York village and nobody denies it, and the piety and philanthropy and culture and philosophy of that village has to be drawed along by that Ring." And sez I, in low but startlin' tones of principle:

"Where, where is it a-drawin' 'em to? Where is it drawin' the hull nation to? Is it drawin' 'em down into a slavery ten times more abject and soul-destroyin' than African slavery ever wuz? Tell me," sez I firmly, "tell me!"

He did not try to frame a reply, he could not find a frame. He knowed it wuz a conundrum boundless as truth and God's justice, and as solemnly deep in its sure consequences of evil as eternity, and as sure to come as that is.

Oh, how solemn he looked, and how sorry I felt for him, for I knowed worse wuz to come, I knowed the sharpest arrow Serepta Pester had sent wuz yet to pierce his sperit. But I sort o' blunted the edge on't what I could conscientiously. Sez I, "I think myself Serepta is a little onreasonable, I myself am willin' to wait three or four weeks. But she's suffered dretful from intemperance from the Rings and from the want of rights, and her sufferin's have made her more voylent in her demands and impatienter," and then I fairly groaned as I did the rest of the errent, and let the sharpest arrow fly from the bo.

"Serepta told me to tell you if you didn't do these errents you should not be President next year."

He trembled like a popple leaf, and I felt that Serepta wuz threatenin' him too hard. Sez he, "I do not wish to be President again, I shall refuse to be nominated. At the same time I dowish to be President and shall work hard for the nomination if you can understand the paradox."

"Yes," sez I, "I understand them paradoxes. I've lived with 'em as you may say, all through my married life."

A clock struck in the next room and I knowed time wuz passin' swift.

Sez the President, "I would be glad to do Serepta's errents, I think she is justified in askin' for her rights, and to have the Ring destroyed, but I am not the one to do them."

Sez I, "Who is the man or men?"

He looked all round the room and up and down as if in hopes he could see someone layin' round on the floor, or danglin' from the ceilin', that would take the responsibility offen him, and in the very nick of time the door opened after a quick rap, and the President jumped up with a relieved look on his linement, and sez:

"Here is the very man to do the errents." And he hastened to introduce me to the Senator who entered. And then he bid me a hasty adoo, but cordial and polite, and withdrew himself.

V

"HE WUZ DRETFUL POLITE"

I felt glad to have this Senator do Serepta's errents, but I didn't like his looks. My land! talk about Serepta Pester bein' disagreeable, he wuz as disagreeable as she any day. He wuz kinder tall and looked out of his eyes and wore a vest. He wuz some bald-headed, and wore a large smile all the while, it looked like a boughten one that didn't fit him, but I won't say it wuz. I presoom he'll be known by this description. But his baldness didn't look to me like Josiah Allen's baldness, and he didn't have the noble linement of the President, no indeed. He wuz dretful polite, good land! politeness is no name for it, but I don't like to see anybody too good. He drawed a chair up for me and himself and asked me:

If he should have the inexpressible honor and delightful joy of aiding me in any way, if so to command him to do it or words to that effect. I can't put down his second-hand smiles and genteel looks and don't want to if I could.

But tacklin' hard jobs as I always tackle 'em, I sot down calm in front of him with my umbrell on my lap and told him all of Serepta's errents, and how I had brought 'em from Jonesville on my tower. I told over all her sufferin's and wrongs from the Rings and from not havin' her rights, and all her sister's Azuba Clapsaddle's, and her Aunt Cassandra Keeler's, and Hulda and Drusilly's and Abagail Flanderses injustices and sufferin's. I did her errents as honorable as I'd love to have one done for me, I told him all the petickulars, and as I finished I said firmly:

"Now can you do Serepta Pesterses errents and will you?"

He leaned forward with that disagreeable boughten smile of hisen and took up one corner of my mantilly, it wuz cut tab fashion, and he took up the tab and said in a low insinuatin' voice, lookin' clost at the edge of the tab:

"Am I mistaken, or is this beautiful creation pipein' or can it be

Kensington tattin'?"

I drawed the tab back coldly and never dained a reply; agin he sez, in a tone of amiable anxiety, "Have I not heard a rumor that bangs are going out of style? I see you do not wear your lovely hair bang-like or a-pompadouris? Ah, women are lovely creatures, lovely beings, every one of 'em." And he sithed, "You are very beautiful," and he sithed agin, a sort of a deceitful lovesick sithe. I sot demute as the Spinks, and a chippin' bird tappin' his wing against her stuny breast would move it jest as much as he moved me by his talk or his sithes. But he kep' on, puttin' on a sort of a sad injured look as if my coldness wuz ondoin' of him.

"My dear madam, it is my misfortune that the topics I introduce, however carefully selected by me, do not seem to be congenial to you. Have you a leanin' toward

Natural history, madam? Have you ever studied into the habits and traits of our American Wad?"

"What?" sez I. For truly a woman's curosity, however parlyzed by just indignation, can stand only just so much strain. "The what?"

"The wad. The animal from which is obtained the valuable fur that tailors make so much use of."

Sez I, "Do you mean waddin' eight cents a sheet?"

"Eight cents a pelt—yes, the skins are plentiful and cheap, owing to the hardy habits of the animal."

Sez I, "Cease instantly. I will hear no more."

Truly, I had heard much of the flattery and little talk statesmen will use to wimmen, and I'd hearn of their lies, etc.; but truly I felt that the half had not been told. And then I thought out-loud and sez:

"I've hearn how laws of eternal right and justice are sot one side in Washington, D.C., as bein' too triflin' to attend to, while the Legislators pondered over and passed laws regardin' hen's eggs and bird's nests. But this is goin' too fur—too fur. But," sez I firmly, "I shall do Serepta's errents, and do 'em to the best of my ability, and you can't draw off my attention from her wrongs and sufferin's by talkin' about wads."

"I would love to obleege Serepta," sez he, "because she belongs to such a lovely sect. Wimmen are the loveliest, most angelic creatures that ever walked the earth; they are perfect, flawless, like snow and roses."

Sez I firmly, "They hain't no such thing; they are disagreeable creeters a good deal of the time. They hain't no better than men, but they ort to have their rights all the same. Now Serepta is disagreeable and kinder fierce actin', and jest as humbly as they make wimmen, but that hain't no sign she ort to be imposed upon; Josiah sez she hadn't ort to have rights she is so humbly, but I don't feel so."

"Who is Josiah?" sez he.

Sez I, "My husband."

"Ah, your husband! Yes, wimmen should have husbands instead of rights. They do not need rights; they need freedom from all cares and sufferin'. Sweet lovely beings! let them have husbands to lift them above all earthly cares and trials! Oh! angels of our homes!" sez he, liftin' his eyes to the heavens and kinder shettin' 'em, some as if he wuz goin' into a spazzum. "Fly around, ye angels, in your native hants; mingle not with rings and vile laws, flee away, flee above them!"

And he kinder waved his hand back and forth in a floatin' fashion up in the air, as if it wuz a woman flyin' up there smooth and serene. It would have impressed some folks dretful, but it didn't me. I sez reasonably:

"Serepta would have been glad to flew above 'em, but the Ring and the vile laws lay holt of her onbeknown to her and dragged her down. And there she is all bruised and broken-hearted by 'em. She didn't meddle with the political Ring, but the Ring meddled with her. How can she fly when the weight of this infamous traffic is holdin' her down?"

"Ahem!" sez he. "Ahem, as it were. As I was saying, my dear madam, these angelic angels of our homes are too ethereal, too dainty to mingle with rude crowds. We political men would fain keep them as they are now; we are willing to stand the rude buffetin' of—of—voting, in order to guard these sweet delicate creatures from any hardships. Sweet tender beings, we would fain guard thee—ah, yes, ah, yes."

Sez I, "Cease instantly, or my sickness will increase, for such talk is like thoroughwort or lobelia to my moral and mental stomach. You know and I know that these angelic tender bein's, half-clothed, fill our streets on icy midnights, huntin' up drunken husbands and fathers and sons. They are driven to death and to moral ruin by the miserable want liquor drinkin' entails. They are starved, they are froze, they are beaten, they are made childless and hopeless by drunken husbands killin' their own flesh and blood. They go down into the cold waves and are drowned by drunken captains; they are cast from railways into death by drunken engineers; they go up on the scaffold and die for crimes committed by the direct aid of this agent of Hell.

"Wimmen had ruther be flyin' round than to do all this, but they can't. If men really believed all they say about wimmen, and I think some on 'em do in a dreamy sentimental way—If wimmen are angels, give 'em the rights of angels. Who ever hearn of a angel foldin' up her wings and goin' to a poor-house or jail through the fault of somebody else? Who ever hearn of a angel bein' dragged off to police court for fightin' to defend her children and herself from a drunken husband that had broke her wings and blacked her eyes, got the angel into the fight and then she got throwed into the streets and imprisoned by it? Who ever hearn of a angel havin' to take in washin' to support a drunken son or father or husband? Who ever hearn of a angel goin' out as wet-nurse to git money to pay taxes on her home to a Govermunt that in theory idolizes her, and practically despises her, and uses that money in ways abominable to that angel. If you want to be consistent, if you're bound to make angels of wimmen, you ort to furnish a free safe place for 'em to soar in. You ort to keep the angels from bein' tormented and bruised and killed, etc."

"Ahem," sez he, "as it were, ahem."

But I kep' right on, for I begun to feel noble and by the side of myself:

"This talk about wimmen bein' outside and above all participation in the laws of her country, is jest as pretty as anything I ever hearn, and jest as simple. Why, you might jest as well throw a lot of snowflakes into the street, and say, 'Some of 'em are female flakes and mustn't be trompled on.' The great march of life tromples on 'em all alike; they fall from one common sky, and are trodden down into one common ground.

"Men and wimmen are made with divine impulses and desires, and human needs and weaknesses, needin' the same heavenly light, and the same human aids and helps. The law should mete out to them the same rewards and punishments.

"Serepta sez you call wimmen angels, and you don't give 'em the rights of the lowest beasts that crawl on the earth. And Serepta told me to tell you that she didn't ask the rights of a angel; she would be perfectly contented and proud, if you would give her the rights of a dog—the assured political rights of a yeller dog.' She said yeller and I'm bound on doin' her 'errent jest as she wanted it done, word for word.

"A dog, Serepta sez, don't have to be hung if it breaks the laws it is not allowed any hand in making; a dog don't have to pay taxes on its bone to a Govermunt that withholds every right of citizenship from it; a dog hain't called undogly if it is industrious and hunts quietly round for its bone to the best of its ability, and tries to git its share of the crumbs that falls from that table bills are laid on.

"A dog hain't preached to about its duty to keep home sweet and sacred, and then see that home turned into a place of danger and torment under laws that these very preachers have made legal and respectable. A dog don't have to see its property taxed to advance laws it believes ruinous, and that breaks its own heart and the heart of other dear dogs. A dog don't have to listen to soul-sickening speeches from them that deny it freedom and justice, about its bein' a damask rose and a seraph, when it knows it hain't; it knows, if it knows anything, that it is jest a plain dog.

"You see Serepta has been embittered by the trials that politics, corrupt legislation have brought right onto her. She didn't want nothin' to do with 'em, but they come onto her onexpected and onbeknown, and she feels that she must do everything she can to alter matters. She wants to help make the laws that have such a overpowerin' influence over her. She believes they can't be much worse than they are now, and may be a little better."

"Ah," interrupted the Senator, "if Serepta wishes to change political affairs, let her influence her children, her boys, and they will carry her benign and noble influence forward into the centuries."

"But the law took her boy, her little boy and girl, away from her. Through the influence of the Whiskey Ring, of which her husband wuz a shinin' member, he got possession of her boy. And so the law has made it perfectly impossible for her to mould it indirectly through him, what Serepta duz she must do herself."

"Ah! my dear woman. A sad thing for Serepta; I trust you have no grievance of this kind, I trust that your estimable husband is, as it were, estimable."

"Yes, Josiah Allen is a good man, as good as men can be. You know men or wimmen can't be only jest about so good anyway. But he's my choice, and he don't drink a drop."

"Pardon me, madam, but if you are happy in your married relations, and your husband is a temperate good man, why do you feel so upon this subject?"

"Why, good land! if you understood the nature of a woman you would know my love for him, my happiness, the content and safety I feel about him and our boy, makes me realize the sufferin's of Serepta in havin' her husband and boy lost to her; makes me realize the depth of a wife's and mother's agony when she sees the one she loves goin' down, down so low she can't reach him; makes me feel how she must yearn to help him in some safe sure way.

"High trees cast long shadows. The happier and more blessed a woman's life is, the more duz she feel for them that are less blessed than she. Highest love goes lowest, like that love that left Heaven and descended to earth, and into it that He might lift up the lowly. The pityin' words of Him who went about pleasin' not Himself, hants me and inspires me; I'm sorry for Serepta, sorry for the hull wimmen race of the nation, and for the men too. Lots of 'em are good creeters, better than wimmen, some on 'em. They want to do right, but don't exactly see the way to do it. In the old slavery times some of the masters wuz more to be pitied than the slaves. They could see the injustice, feel the wrong they wuz doin', but old chains of Custom bound 'em, social customs and idees had hardened into habits of thought.

"They realized the size and heft of the evil, but didn't know how to grapple with it, and throw it. So now, many men see the evils of this time, want to help, but don't know the best way to lay holt of 'em. Life is a curious conundrum anyway, and hard to guess. But we can try to git the right answer to it as fur as we can. Serepta feels that one of the answers to the conundrum is in gittin' her rights. I myself have got all the rights I need or want, as fur as my own happiness is concerned. My home is my castle (a story and a half wooden one, but dear). My towers elevate me, the companionship of my friends give social happiness, our children are prosperous and happy. We have property enough for all the comforts of life. And above all other things my Josiah is my love and my theme."

"Ah, yes!" sez he, "love is a woman's empire, and in that she should find her full content—her entire happiness and thought. A womanly woman will not look outside that lovely and safe and beautious empire."

Sez I firmly, "If she hain't a idiot she can't help it. Love is the most beautiful thing on earth, the most holy and satisfyin'. But I do not ask you as a politician, but as a human bein', which would you like best, the love of a strong, earnest tender nature, for in man or woman 'the strongest are the tenderest, the loving are the daring,' which would you like best, the love and respect of such a nature full of wit, of tenderness, of infinite variety, or the love of a fool?

"A fool's love is wearin', it is insipid at best, and it turns to vinegar. Why, sweetened water must turn to vinegar, it is its nater. And if a woman is bright and true-hearted, she can't help seein' through an injustice. She may be happy in her own home. Domestic affection, social enjoyments, the delights of a cultured home and society, and the companionship of the man she loves and who loves her, will, if she is a true woman, satisfy her own personal needs and desires, and she would far ruther for her own selfish happiness rest quietly in that love, that most blessed home.

"But the bright quick intellect that delights you can't help seein' an injustice, can't help seein' through shams of all kinds, sham sentiment, sham compliments, sham justice. The tender lovin' nature that blesses your life can't help feelin' pity for them less blessed than herself. She looks down through the love-guarded lattice of her home from which your care would fain bar out all sights of woe and squaler, she looks down and sees the weary toilers below, the hopeless, the wretched. She sees the steep hills they have to climb, carryin' their crosses, she sees 'em go down into the mire, dragged there by the love that should lift 'em up. She would not be the woman you love if she could restrain her hand from liftin' up the fallen, wipin' tears from weepin' eyes, speakin' brave words for them that can't speak for themselves. The very strength of her affection that would hold you up if you were in trouble or disgrace yearns to help all sorrowin' hearts.

"Down in your heart you can't help admirin' her for this, we can't help respectin' the one that advocates the right, the true, even if they are our conquerors. Wimmen hain't angels; now to be candid, you know they hain't. They hain't any better than men. Men are considerable likely; and it seems curious to me that they should act so in this one thing. For men ort to be more honest and open than wimmen. They hain't had to cajole and wheedle and use little trickeries and deceits and indirect ways as wimmen have. Why, cramp a tree limb and see if it will grow as straight and vigorous as it would in full freedom and sunshine.

"Men ort to be nobler than women, sincerer, braver. And they ort to be ashamed of this one trick of theirn, for they know they hain't honest in it, they hain't generous. Give wimmen two or three generations of moral and legal freedom and see if men will laugh at 'em for their little deceits and affectations. No, men will be gentler, and wimmen nobler, and they will both come nearer bein' angels, though most probable they won't be any too good then, I hain't a mite afraid of it."

VI

"CONCERNING MOTH-MILLERS AND MINNY FISH"

The Senator kinder sithed, and that sithe sort o' brought me down onto my feet agin as it were, and a sense of my duty, and I spoke out agin:

"Can you and will you do Serepta's errents?"

He evaded a direct answer by sayin', "As you alluded to the little indirect ways of women, dearest madam, you will pardon me for saying that it is my belief that the soft gentle brains of females are unfitted for the deep hard problems men have to grapple with. They are too doll-like, too angelically and sweetly frivolous."

"No doubt," sez I, "some wimmen are frivolous and some men foolish, for as Mrs. Poyser said, 'God made women to match the men,' but these few hadn't ort to disfranchise the hull race of men and wimmen. And as to soft brains, Maria Mitchell discovered planets hid from masculine eyes from the beginnin' of time, and do you think that wimmen can't see the black spots on the body politic, that darkens the life of her and her children?

"Madame Curie discovered the light that looks through solid wood and iron, and you think wimmen can't see through unjust laws and practices, the rampant evils of to-day, and see what is on the other side, see a remedy for 'em. Florence Nightingale could mother and help cure an army, and why hain't men willin' to let wimmen help cure a sick legislation, kinder mother it, and encourage it to do better? She might much better be doin' that, than playin' bridge-whist, or rastlin' with hobble skirts, and it wouldn't devour any more time."

He sot demute for a few minutes and then he sez, "While on the subject of women's achievements, dearest madam, allow me to ask you, if they have reached the importance you claim for them, why is it that so few women are made immortal by bein' represented in the Hall of Fame? And why are the four or five females represented there put away by themselves in a remote unadorned corner with no roof to protect them from the rough winds and storms that beat upon them?"

Sez I, "That's a good illustration of what I've been sayin'. It wuz owin' to a woman's gift that America has a Hall of Fame, and it would seem that common courtesy would give wimmen an equally desirable place amongst the Immortals. Do you spoze that if women formed half the committee of selection—which they should since it wuz a woman's gift that made such a place possible—do you spoze that if she had an equal voice with men, the names of noble wimmen would be tucked away in a remote unroofed corner?

"Edgar Allan Poe's genius wuz worthy a place among the Immortals, no doubt; his poems and stories excite wonder and admiration. But do they move the soul like

Mrs. Stowe's immortal story that thrilled the world and helped free a race? — yes, two races — for the curse of slavery held the white race in bondage, too. Yet she and her three or four woman companions face the stormy winds in an out-of-the-way corner, while Poe occupies his honorable sightly place among his fifty or more male companions.

"Wimmen have always been admonished to not strive for right and justice but to lean on men's generosity and chivalry. Here wuz a place where that chivalry would have shone, but it didn't seem to materialize, and if wimmen had leaned on it, it would have proved a weak staff, indeed.

"Such things as this are constantly occurring and show plain that wimmen needs the ballot to protect her from all sorts of wrongs and indignities. Men take wimmen's money, as they did here, and use it to uplift themselves, and lower her, like taxin' her heavily and often unjustly and usin' this money to help forward unjust laws which she abominates. And so it goes on, and will, until women are men's equals legally and politically."

"Ahem — you present things in a new light. I never looked at this matter with your eyes."

"No, you looked at 'em through a man's eyes; such things are so customary that men do 'em without thinkin', from habit and custom, like hushin' up children's talk, when they interrupt grown-ups."

Agin he sot demute for a short space, and then said, "I feel that natural human instinct is aginst the change. In savage races that knew nothin' of civilization, male force and strength always ruled."

"Why," sez I, "history tells us of savage races where wimmen always rule, though I don't think they ort to — ability and goodness ort to rule."

"Nature is aginst it," sez he.

But I sez firmly, "Bees and lots of other insects and animals always have a female for queen and ruler. They rule blindly and entirely, right on through the centuries, but we are enlightened and should not encourage it. In my opinion the male bee has just as good a right to be monarch as his female pardner has, if he is as good and knows as much. I never believed in the female workin' ones killin' off the male drones to save winterin' 'em; they might give 'em some light chores to do round the hive to pay for their board. I love justice and that would be my way."

Agin he sithed. "Modern history don't seem to favor the scheme —" But his axent wuz as weak as a cat and his boughten smile seemed crackin' and wearin' out; he knowed better.

Sez I, "We won't argy long on that p'int, for I might overwhelm you if I approved of overwhelmin', but, will merely ask you to cast one eye on England. Was the rain of Victoria the Good less peaceful and prosperous than that of the male rulers who preceded her? And you can then throw your other eye over to Holland: is their sweet queen less worthy and beloved to-day than other European monarchs? And is her throne more shaky and tottlin' than theirn?"

He didn't try to dispute me and bowed his head on his breast in a almost meachin' way. He knowed he wuz beat on every side, and almost to the end of his chain of rusty, broken old arguments. But anon he brightened up agin and sez, ketchin' holt of the last shackly link of his argument:

"You seem to place a great deal of dependence on the Bible. The Bible is aginst the idee. The Bible teaches man's supremacy, man's absolute power and might and authority."

"Why, how you talk," sez I. "In the very first chapter the Bible tells how man wuz turned right round by a woman, tells how she not only turned man round to do as she wanted him to, but turned the hull world over.

"That hain't nothin' I approve of; I don't speak of it because I like the idee. That wuzn't done in a open honorable manner as things should be done. No, Eve ruled by indirect influence, the gently influencing men way, that politicians are so fond of. And she brought ruin and destruction onto the hull world by it.

"A few years later when men and wimmen grew wiser, when we hear of wimmen rulin' Israel openly and honestly, like Miriam, Deborah and other likely old four mothers, things went on better. They didn't act meachin' and tempt, and act indirect."

He sithed powerful and sot round oneasy in his chair. And sez he, "I thought wimmen wuz taught by the Bible to serve and love their homes."

"So they be. And every true woman loves to serve. Home is my supreme happiness and delight, and my best happiness is found in servin' them I love. But I must tell the truth, in the house or outdoors."

Sez he faintly, "The Old Testament may teach that women have some strength and power. But in the New Testament in every great undertaken' and plan men have been chosen by God to carry them through."

"Why-ee!" sez I, "how you talk! Have you ever read the Bible?"

He said evasively, his grandmother owned one, and he had seen it in early youth. And then he went on in a sort of apologizin' way. He had always meant to read it, but he had entered political life at an early age where the Bible wuzn't popular, and he believed that he had never read further than the Epistles of Gulliver to the Liliputians.

Sez I, "That hain't Bible, there hain't no Gulliver in it, and you mean

Galatians."

Well, he said, that might be it, it wuz some man he knew, and he had always heard and believed that man wuz the only worker that God had chosen.

"Why," sez I, "the one great theme of the New Testament—the salvation of the world through the birth of Christ—no man had anything to do with. Our divine Lord wuz born of God and Woman. Heavenly plan of redemption for fallen humanity. God Himself called woman into that work, the divine work of saving a world, and why shouldn't she continue in it? God called her. Mary had no dream of publicity, no desire of a world's work of suffering and renunciation. The soft air of Galilee wropped her about in its sweet content, as she dreamed her quiet dreams in maiden peace—dreamed, perhaps, of domestic love and happiness.

"From that sweetest silence, the restful peace of happy innocent girlhood, God called her to her divine work of helpin' redeem a world from sin. And did not this woman's love and willin' obedience, and sufferin' set her apart, baptize her for this work of liftin' up the fallen, helpin' the weak?

"Is it not a part of woman's life that she gave at the birth and crucifixion? Her faith, her hope, her sufferin', her glow of divine pity and joyful martyrdom. These, mingled with the divine, the pure heavenly, have they not for nineteen hundred years been blessin' the world? The God in Christ would awe us too much; we would shield our eyes from the too blindin' glory of the pure God-like. But the tender Christ who wept over a sinful city, and the grave of His friend, who stopped dyin' on the cross to comfort His mother's heart, provide for her future—it is this womanly element in our Lord's nature that makes us dare to approach Him, dare to kneel at His feet?

"And since woman wuz so blessed as to be counted worthy to be co-worker with God in the beginnin' of the world's redemption; since He called her from the quiet obscurity of womanly rest and peace into the blessed martyrdom of renunciation and toil and sufferin', all to help a world that cared nothin' for her, that cried out shame upon her.

"He will help her carry on the work of helpin' a sinful world. He will protect her in it, she cannot be harmed or hindered, for the cause she loves of helpin' men and wimmen, is God's cause too, and God will take care of His own. Herods full of greed and frightened selfishness may try to break her heart by efforts to kill the child she loves, but she will hold it so clost to her bosom he can't destroy it; and the light of the Divine will go before her, showin' the way through the desert and wilderness mebby, but she shall bear it into safety."

"You spoke of Herod," sez he dreamily, "the name sounds familiar to me. Was not Mr. Herod once in the United States Senate?"

"Not that one," sez I. "He died some time ago, but I guess he has relatives there now, judgin' from laws made there. You ask who Herod wuz, and as it all seems a new story to you, I will tell you. When the Saviour of the world wuz born in Bethlehem, and a woman wuz tryin' to save His life, a man by the name of Herod wuz tryin' his best out of selfishness and greed to murder Him."

"Ah! that was not right in Herod."

"No, it hain't been called so. And what wuzn't right in him hain't right in his relations who are tryin' to do the same thing to-day. Sellin' for money the right to destroy the child the mother carries on her heart. Surroundin' him with temptations so murderous, yet so enticin' to youthful spirits, that the mother feels that as the laws are now, the grave is the only place of safety that God Himself can find for her boy. But because Herod wuz so mean it hain't no sign that all men are mean. Joseph wuz as likely as he could be."

"Joseph?" sez he pensively. "Do you allude to our venerable speaker, Joe

Cannon?"

"No," sez I. "I'm talkin' Bible—I'm talkin' about Joseph; jest plain

Joseph."

"Ah! I see. I am not fully familiar with that work. Being so engrossed in politics, and political literature, I don't git any time to devote to less important publications."

Sez I candidly, "I knew you hadn't read it the minute you mentioned the book of Liliputians. But as I wuz sayin', Joseph wuz a likely man. He had the strength to lead the way, overcome obstacles, keep dangers from Mary, protect her tenderer form with the mantilly of his generous devotion.

"But she carried the Child on her bosom; ponderin' high things in her heart that Joseph never dreamed of. That is what is wanted now, and in the future. The man and the woman walkin' side by side. He a little ahead, mebby, to keep off dangers by his greater strength and courage. She a-carryin' the infant Christ of Love, bearin' the baby Peace in her bosom, carryin' it into safety from them that seek to destroy it.

"And as I said before, if God called woman into this work, He will enable her to carry it through. He will protect her from her own weaknesses, and the misapprehensions and hard judgments and injustices of a gain-sayin' world.

"Yes, the star of hope is risin' in the sky brighter and brighter, and wise men are even now comin' to the mother of the new Redeemer, led by the star."

He sot demute. Silence rained for some time; and finally I spoke out solemnly through the rain:

"Will you do Serepta's errents? Will you give her her rights? And will you break the Whiskey Ring?"

He said he would love to do the errents, I had convinced him that it would be just and right to do 'em, but the Constitution of the United States stood up firm aginst 'em. As the laws of the United States wuz, he could not make any move toward doin' either of the errents.

Sez I, "Can't the laws be changed?"

"Be changed? Change the laws of the United States? Tamper with the glorious

Constitution that our fore-fathers left us — an immortal sacred legacy."

He jumped up on his feet and his second-hand smile fell off. He kinder shook as if he wuz skairt most to death and tremblin' with horror. He did it to skair me, I knew, but I knowed I meant well towards the Constitution and our old forefathers; and my principles stiddied me and held me firm and serene. And when he asked me agin in tones full of awe and horror:

"Can it be that I heard my ear aright? Or did you speak of changin' the unalterable laws of the United States — tampering with the Constitution?"

"Yes, that is what I said. Hain't they never been changed?"

He dropped that skairful look and put on a firm judicial one. He see that he could not skair me to death; an' sez he, "Oh, yes, they've been changed in cases of necessity."

Sez I, "For instance durin' the Oncivil war it wuz changed to make Northern men cheap bloodhounds and hunters."

"Yes," he said, "it seemed to be a case of necessity and economy."

"I know it," sez I; "men wuz cheaper than any other breed of bloodhounds the slave-holders could employ to hunt men and wimmen with, and more faithful."

"Yes," he said, "it wuz a case of clear economy."

And sez I: "The laws have been changed to benefit liquor dealers."

"Well, yes," he said, "it had been changed to enable whiskey dealers to utilize the surplus liquor they import."

Sez he, gittin' kinder animated, for he wuz on a congenial and familar theme, "Nobody, the best calculators in drunkards, can exactly calculate how much whiskey will be drunk in a year; and so, ruther than have the whiskey dealers suffer loss, the law had to be changed. And then," sez he, growin' still more candid in his excitement, "we are makin' a powerful effort to change the laws now so as to take the tax off of whiskey, so it can be sold cheaper, and obtained in greater quantities by the masses. Any such great laws would justify a change in the Constitution and the laws; but for any frivolous cause, any trivial cause, madam, we male custodians of the sacred Constitution stand as walls of iron before it, guarding it from any shadow of change. Faithful we will be, faithful unto death."

Sez I, "As it has been changed, it can be agin. And you jest said I had convinced you that Serepta's errents wuz errents of truth and justice, and you would love to do 'em."

"Well, yes, yes—I would love to—as it were—. But, my dear madam, much as

I would like to oblige you, I have not the time to devote to the cause of

Right and Justice. I don't think you realize the constant pressure of hard

work that is ageing us and wearing us out, before our day.

"As I said, we have to watch the liquor interest constantly to see that the liquor dealers suffer no loss—we have to do that, of course."

And he continued dreamily, as if losin' sight of me and talkin' to himself: "The wealthy Corporations and Trusts, we have to condemn them loudly to please the common people, and help 'em secretly to please ourselves, or our richest perkisits are lost. The Canal Ring, the Indian Agency, the Land Grabbers, the political bosses. In fact, we are surrounded by a host of bandits that we have to appease and profit by; oh, how these matters wear into the gray matter of our brains!"

"Gray matter!" sez I, with my nose uplifted to its extremest height, "I should call it black matter!"

"Well, the name is immaterial, but these labors, though pocket filling, are brain wearing. And of late I and the rest of our loyal henchmen have been worn out in our labors in tariff revision. You know how we claim to help the common people by the revision; you've probable read about it in the papers."

"Yes," sez I coldly, "I've hearn talk."

"Yes," sez he, "but if we do succeed, after the most strenuous efforts in getting the duty off champagne, green turtle, olives, etc., and put on to sugar, tea, cotton cloth and such like, with all this brain fag and brain labor—"

"And tongue labor!" sez I in a icy axent.

"Yes, after all this ceaseless toil the common people will not show any gratitude; we statesmen labor oft with aching hearts." And he leaned his forward on his hand and sithed.

But my looks wuz like ice-suckles on the north side of a barn. And I stopped his complaints and his sithes by askin' in a voice that demanded a reply:

"Can you and will you do Serepta's errents? Errents full of truth and justice and eternal right?"

He said he knew they wuz jest runnin' over with them qualities, but happy as it would make him to do 'em, he had to refuse owin' to the fur more important matters he had named, and the many, many other laws and preambles that he hadn't time to name over to me. "Mebby you have heard," sez he, "that we are now engaged in making most important laws concerning moth-millers, and minny fish, and hog cholera. And take it with these important bills and the constant strain on our minds in tryin' to pass laws to increase our own salaries, you can see jest how cramped we are for time. And though we would love to pass some laws of truth and righteousness—we fairly ache to—yet not havin' the requisite time we are forced to lay 'em on the table or under it."

"Well," sez I, "I guess I may as well be a-goin'." And I bid him a cool goodbye and started for the door. But jest as my hand wuz on the nub he jumped up and opened the door, wearin' that boughten second-hand smile agin on his linement, and sez he:

"Dear madam, perhaps Senator B. will do the errents for you."

Sez I, "Where is Senator B.?" And he said I would find him at his Post of

Duty at the Capitol.

"Well," I said, "I will hunt up the Post," and did. A grand enough place for a Emperor or a Zar is the Capitol of our great nation where I found him, a good natured lookin' boy in buttons showin' me the Post.

VII

"NO HAMPERIN' HITCHIN' STRAPS"

Well, Senator B. wanted to do the errents but said it wuz not his place, and sent me to Senator C., and he almost cried, he wanted to do 'em so bad, but stern duty tied him to his Post, he said, and he sent me to Senator D., and he did cry onto his handkerchief, he wanted to do the errents so bad, and said it would be such a good thing to have 'em done. He bust right into tears as he said he had to refuse to do 'em. Whether they wuz wet tears or dry ones I couldn't tell, his handkerchief wuz so big, but I hearn his sithes, and they wuz deep and powerful ones.

But as I sez to him, "Wet tears, nor dry ones, nor windy sithes didn't help do the errents." So I went on his sobbin' advice to Senator E., and he wuz huffy and didn't want to do 'em and said so. And said his wife had thirteen children, and wimmen instead of votin' ort to go and do likewise.

And I told him it wouldn't look well in onmarried wimmen and widders, and if they should foller her example folks would talk.

And he said, "They ort to marry."

And I said, "As the fashion is now, wimmen had to wait for some man to ask 'em, and if they didn't come up to the mark and ask 'em, who wuz to blame?"

He wouldn't answer, and looked sulky, but honest, and wouldn't tell me who to go to to git the errents done.

But jest outside his door I met the Senator I had left sobbin' over the errents. He looked real hilarious, but drawed his face down when he ketched my eye, and sithed several times, and sent me to Senator F. and he sent me to Senator G.

And suffice it to say I wuz sent round, and talked to, and cried at, and sulked to, and smiled at and scowled at, and encouraged and discouraged, 'till my head swum and my knees wobbled under me. And with all my efforts and outlay of oratory and shue leather not one of Serepta Pester's errents could I git done, and no hopes held out of their ever bein' done. And about the middle of the afternoon I gin up, there wuz no use in tryin' any longer and I turned my weary tracks towards the outside door. But as bad as I felt, I couldn't help my sperit bein' lifted up some by the grandeur about me.

Oh, my land! to stand in the immense hall and look up, and up, and see all the colors of the rain-bow and see what wonderful pictures there wuz up there in the sky above me as it were. Why, it seemed curiouser than any Northern lights I ever see in my life, and they stream up dretful curious sometimes. And as I walked through that lofty and most beautiful place and realized the size and majestic proportions of the buildin' I wondered to myself that a small law, a little unjust law could ever be passed in such grand and magnificent surroundin's. And I sez to myself, it can't be the fault of the place anyway; the law-makers have a chance for their souls to soar if they want to, here is room and to spare to pass laws big as elephants and camels, and I wondered that they should ever try to pass laws as small as muskeeters and nats. Thinkses I, I wonder them little laws don't git to strollin' round and git lost in them magnificent corridors. But I consoled myself, thinkin' it wouldn't be no great loss if they did. But right here, as I wuz thinkin' on these deep and lofty subjects, I met the good natured young chap that had showed me round and he sez:

"You look fatigued, mom." (Soarin' even to yourself is tuckerin'.) "You look very fatigued; won't you take something?"

I looked at him with a curious silent sort of a look; for I didn't know what he meant. Agin he looked clost at me and sort o' pityin'; and sez he, "You look tired out, mom. Won't you take something? Let me treat you to something; what will you take, mom?"

I thought he wuz actin' dretful liberal, but I knew they had strange ways in Washington anyway. And I didn't know but it wuz their way to make some present to every woman that comes there, and I didn't want to act awkward and out of style, so I sez:

"I don't want to take anything, and don't see any reason why you should insist on't. But if I have got to take sunthin' I had jest as soon have a few yards of factory cloth as anything. That always comes handy."

I thought that if he wuz determined to treat me to show his good feelin's towards me, I would git sunthin' useful and that would do me some good, else what wuz the good of bein' treated? And I thought that if I had got to take a present from a strange man, I would make a shirt for Josiah out of it. I thought that would save jealousy and make it right so fur as goodness went.

"But," sez he, "I mean beer or wine or liquor of some kind."

I riz right up in my shues and dignity, and glared at him.

Sez he, "There is a saloon right here handy in the buildin'."

Sez I in awful axents, "It is very appropriate to have it here handy!" Sez I, "Liquor duz more towards makin' the laws of the United States from Caucus to Convention than anything else duz, and it is highly proper to have it here so they can soak the laws in it right off before they lay 'em onto the table or under 'em, or pass 'em onto the people. It is highly appropriate," sez I.

"Yes," sez he. "It is very handy for the Senators and Congressmen, and let me get you a glass."

"No, you won't!" sez I firmly. "The nation suffers enough from that room now without havin' Josiah Allen's wife let in."

Sez he, "If you have any feeling of delicacy in goin' in there, let me make some wine here. I will get a glass of water and make you some pure grape wine, or French brandy, or corn or rye whiskey. I have all the drugs right here." And he took a little box out of his pocket. "My father is a importer of rare old wines, and I know just how it is done. I have 'em all here, Capsicum, Coculus Indicus, alum, copperas, strychnine; I will make some of the choicest, oldest, and purest imported liquors we have in the country, in five minutes if you say so."

"No!" sez I firmly, "when I want to foller Cleopatra's fashion and commit suicide, I will hire a rattlesnake and take my pizen as she did, on the outside."

Well, I got back to Hiram Cagwin's tired as a dog, and Serepta's errents ondone. But my conscience opholded me and told me I had done my very best, and man or woman can do no more.

Well, the next day but one wuz the big outdoor suffrage meetin'. And we sot off in good season, Hiram feelin' well enough to be left with the hired help. Polly started before we did with some of her college mates, lookin' pretty as a pink with a red rose pinned over a achin' heart, so I spoze, for she loved the young man who wuz out with another girl May-flowering. Burnin' zeal and lofty principle can't take the place in a woman's heart of love and domestic happiness, and men needn't be afraid it will. There is no more danger on't than there is of a settin' hen wantin' to leave her nest to be a commercial traveler. Nature has made laws for wimmen and hens that no ballot, male or female, can upset.

Josiah and Lorinda and I went in the trolley in good season, so's to git a sightly place, Lorinda protestin' all the time aginst the indelicacy and impropriety of wimmen's appearin' in outdoor meetin's, forgittin', I spose, the dense procession of wimmen that fills the avenues every day, follerin' Fashion and Display. As nigh as I could make out the impropriety consisted in wimmen's follerin' after Justice and Right.

Josiah's face looked dubersome. I guess he wuz worryin' over his offer to represent me, and thinkin' of Aunt Susan and the twins.

But as it turned out I met Diantha while Josiah wuz in a shop buyin' some peppermint lozengers, and she said her niece had come from the West, and they got along all right. So that lifted my burden. But I thought best not to tell Josiah, as he wuz so bound to represent me. I thought it wouldn't do any hurt to let him think it over about the job a man took on himself when he sot out to represent a woman. They wouldn't like it in lots of ways, as willin' as they seem to be in print.

Wimmen go through lots of things calm and patient that would make a man flinch and shy off like a balky horse, and visey versey. I wouldn't want to represent Josiah lots of times, breakin' colts, ploughin' greensward, cuttin' cord-wood etc., etc. Men and wimmen want equal legal rights to represent themselves and their own sex which are different, and always must be, and both sexes don't want to be hampered and sot down on by the other one. That is gauldin' to human nater, male or female.

We got a good place nigh the speakers' stand, and we hadn't stood there long before the parade hove in sight, the yeller banners streamin' out like sunshine on a rainy day, police outriders, music, etc.

More than a hundred automobiles led the parade and five times as many wimmen walkin' afoot. A big grand-stand with the lady speakers and their friends on it, all dressed pretty as pinks. For the old idee that suffragists don't care for attractive dress and domestic life wuz exploded long ago, and many other old superstitions went up in the blaze.

Those of us who have gray hair can remember when if a man spoke favorably of women's rights the sarcastic question was asked him: "How old is Susan B. Anthony?"

And this fine wit and cuttin' ridicule would silence argument and quench the spirit of the upholder.

But the world moves. Susan's memory is beloved and revered, and the contemptious ridicule of the onthinkin' and ignorant only nourished the laurels the world lays on her tomb.

At that time accordin' to popular opinion a suffragist wuz a slatternly woman with uncombed locks, dangling shoe strings, and bloomers, stridin' through an unswept house onmindful of dirty children or hungry husband, but the world moves onward and public opinion with it. Suffragists are the best mothers, the best housekeepers, the best dressers of any wimmen in the land. Search the records and you'll find it so, and why?

Because they know sunthin', it takes common sense to make a gooseberry pie as it ort to be. And the more a woman knows and the more justice she demands, the better for her husband. The same sperit that rebels at tyranny and injustice rebels at dirt, disorder, discomfort, and all unpleasant conditions.

I looked ahead with my mind's eye and see them pretty college girls settled down in pleasant homes of their own, where sanitary laws prevailed, where the babies wuzn't fed pickles and cabbage, and kep' in air-tight enclosures. Where the husbands did not have to go outside their own homes to find cheer and comfort, and intelligent conversation, and where Love and Common Sense walked hand in hand toward Happiness and Contentment, Justice, with her blinders offen her eyes, goin' ahead on 'em. I never liked the idee of Justice wearin' them bandages over her eyes. She ort to have both eyes open; if anybody ever needed good eyesight she duz, to choose the straight and narrer road, lookin' backward to see the mistakes she has made in the past, so's to shun 'em in the future, and lookin' all round her in the present to see where she can help matters, and lookin' fur off in the future to the bright dawn of a Tomorrow. To the shinin' mount of Equal Rights and full Liberty. Where she sees men and wimmen standin' side by side with no halters or hamperin' hitchin' straps on either on 'em. He more gentle and considerate, and she less cowardly and emotional.

Good land! what could Justice do blind in one eye and wimmen on the blind side? But good sensible wimmen are reachin' up and pullin' the bandages offen her eyes. She's in a fair way to git her eyesight. But I'm eppisodin', and to resoom forward.

VIII

"OLD MOM NATER LISTENIN'"

There wuz some pleasant talkin' and jokin' between bystanders and suffragettes, and then some good natured but keen and sensible speeches. And one pretty speaker told about the doin's at Albany and Washington. How women's respectful pleas for justice are treated there. How the law-makers, born and nussed by wimmen and dependent on 'em for comfort and happiness, use the wimmen's tax money to help make laws makin' her of no legal importance only as helpless figgers to hang taxation and punishment on.

Old Mom Nater had been listenin' clost, her sky-blue eyes shinin' with joy to see her own sect present such a noble appearance in the parade. But when these insults and indignities wuz brung up to her mind agin and she realized afresh how wimmen couldn't git no more rights accorded to her than a dog or a hen, and worse. For a hen or a dog wouldn't be taxed to raise money for turkle soup and shampain to nourish the law-makers whilst they made the laws agin 'em—Mom Nater's eyes clouded over with indignation and resentment, and she boo-hooed right out a-cryin'. Helpless tears, of no more account than other females have shed, and will, as they set on their hard benches with idiots, lunaticks, and criminals.

Of course she wiped up her tears pretty soon, not willin' to lose any of the wimmen's bright speeches. But when her tear-drops fell fast, Josiah sez to me, "You'll see them wimmen run like hikers now, wimmen always thought more of shiffon and fol-de-rols than they did of principle."

But I sez, "Wait and see," (we wuz under a awnin' and protected).

But the young and pretty speaker who wore a light silk dress and exquisite bunnet, kep' right on talkin' jest as calmly as if she didn't know her pretty dress wuz bein' spilte and her bunnet gittin' wet as sop, and I sez to Josiah:

"When wimmen are so in earnest, and want anything so much they can stand soakin' in their best dresses, and let their Sunday bunnets be spilte on their heads, not noticin' 'em seemin'ly, but keep right on pleadin' for right and justice, they are in a fair way of gittin' what they are after."

He looked kinder meachin' but didn't dispute me.

The speeches wuz beautiful and convincin', and pretty soon old Mom Nater stopped cryin' to hear 'em, and she and I both listened full of joy and happiness to see with what eloquence and justice our sect wuz pleadin' our cause. Their arguments wuz so reasonable and convincin' that I said to myself, I don't see how anybody can help bein' converted to this righteous cause, the liftin' up of wimmen from her uncomfortable crouchin' poster with criminals and idiots, up to the place she should occupy by the side of other good citizens of the United States, with all the legal and moral rights that go with that noble title.

And right whilst I wuz thinkin' this, sunthin' wuz happenin' that proved I wuz right in my eppisodin', and somebody awful sot agin it wuz bein' converted then and there (but of this more anon and bom-bye). We stayed till we heard the last word of the last speech, I happy and proud in sperit, Lorinda partly converted, she couldn't help it, though she wouldn't own up to it at that juncter. And Josiah lookin' real deprested, the thought of representin' me wuz worryin' him I knew, for I hearn him say (soty vosy), "Represent wimmen or not, I hain't goin' to set up all night with no old woman, and lift her round, nor dry nuss no twins."

And thinkin' his sperit wuz pierced to a sufficient depth by his apprehension, so reason could be planted and take root, and he wouldn't be so anxious in the future to represent a woman, I told him what Diantha said and we all went home in good sperits. The sun shone clear, the rain had washed the face of the Earth till it shone, and everything looked gay and joyous.

When we got to Lorinda's we see a auto standin' in front of the door full of flowery branches in front and the pink posies lookin' no more bright and rosy than the faces of the two young folks settin' there. It wuz Polly and Royal.

It seemed that when he and Maud got back from the country (and they didn't stay long, Royal wuz so restless and oneasy) Maud insisted on his takin' her to the suffrage meetin' jest to make fun on't, so I spoze. She thought she had rubbed out Polly's image and made a impression herself on Royal's heart that only needed stompin' in a little deeper, and she thought ridicule would be the stomper she needed.

But when they got to the meetin' and he see Polly settin' like a lily amongst flowers, and read in her lovely face the earnest desire to lift the burden from the heavy laden, comfort the sorrowful, right the wrong, and do what she could in her day and generation —

I spoze his eyes could only see her sweet face. But he couldn't help his ears from hearin' the reasonable, eloquent words of earnest and womanly wimmen, so full of good sense and truth and justice that no reasonable person could dispute 'em, and when he contrasted all this with the sneerin' face, the sarcastic egotistic prattle of Maud, the veil dropped from his eyes, and he see with the New Vision.

You know how it wuz with Saul the Scoffer who went breathin' out vengeance, and Eternal Right stopped him on his way with its great light. Well, I spoze it wuz a bright ray from that same light that shone down into Royal's heart and made him see. He wuz always good hearted and generous — men have always been better than the laws they have made. He left Maud at her home not fur away and hastened back, way-laid Polly, and bore her home in triumph and a thirty-horse-power car.

It don't make much difference I spoze how or where anybody is converted. The Bible speaks of some bein' ketched out of the fire, and I spoze it is about the same if they are ketched out of the rain. 'Tennyrate the same rain that washed some of the color off Maud's cheeks, seemed to wash away the blindin' mist of prejudice and antagonism from Royal's mental vision, leavin' his sperit ready for the great white light of truth and justice to strike in. And that very day and hour he come round to Polly's way of thinkin', and bein' smart as a whip and so rich, I suppose he will be a great accusation to the cause.

Well, the next day but one the Allens met in a pleasant grove on the river shore and we had a good growin' time. Royal bein' as you may say one of the family, took us all to the grove in his big tourin' car, and the fourth trip he took Polly alone, and wuzn't it queer that, though the load wuz fur lighter, it took him three times as long as the other three trips together? Why, they never got there till dinner wuz on the table, and then they didn't seem to care a mite about the extra good food.

But I made allowances, for as I looked into their glowin' faces I knowed they wuz partakin' of fruit from the full branches of first love, true love. Rich fruit that gives the divinest satisfaction of any this old earth affords. Food that never changes through the centuries, though fashion often changes, and riotous plenty or food famine may exalt or depress the sperit of the householder. Nothin' but time has any power over this divine fruitage. He gradually, as the light of the honeymoon wanes, whets his old scythe and mows down some of the luxuriant branches, either cuttin' a full swath, or one at a time, and the blessed consumers have to come down to the ordinary food of mortals. But this wuz still fur away from them.

And I knowed too that the ordinary food of ordinary mortals partook of under the full harvest moon of domestic comfort and contentment wuz not to be despised, though fur different. And the light fur different from the glow and the glamour that wropped them two together and all the rest of the world away from 'em.

But I'm eppisodin' too much, and to resoom forward.

As I said, we had a happy growin' time at the Reunion, Josiah bein' in fine feather to see the relation on his side presentin' such a noble appearance. And like a good wife I sympathized with him in his pride and happiness, though I told him they didn't present any better appearance than the same number of Smiths would. And their cookin', though excellent, wuz no better than the Smiths could cook if they sot out to.

He bein' so good natered didn't dispute me outright, but said he thought the Allens made better nut-cakes than the Smiths.

But they don't, no such thing. In fact I think the Smith nut-cakes are lighter and have a more artistic twist to 'em and don't devour so much fat a-fryin'.

But I'd hate to set Josiah down to any better vittles. I d'no as I would dast let him loose at the table at a Smith reunion, for he eat fur too much as it wuz. I had to give him five pepsin lozengers and some pepper tea. And then I looked out all night for night mairs to ride on his chist. But he come through it alive though with considerable pain.

We stayed two or three days longer with Lorinda, and then she and Hiram went part way with us as we visited our way home. We've got relations livin' all along the river that we owed visits to. And we went to see a number of 'em and enjoyed our four selves first rate. These things all took place more than a year ago and another man sets in the high chair, before which I laid Serepta's errents, a man not so hefty mebby weighed by common steelyards, but one of noble weight judged by mental and moral scales.

I d'no whether I'd had any better luck if I'd presented Serepta's errents to him. Sometimes when I look in the kind eyes of his picter, and read his noble and eloquent words that I believe come from his very soul, I think mebby I'd been more lucky if he'd sot in the chair that day. But then I d'no, there are so many influences and hendrances planted like thorns in the cushion of that chair that a man, no matter how earnest he strives to do jest right, can't help bein' pricked by 'em and held back. And I know he could never done them errents in the time she sot, but I'm in hopes he'll throw his powerful influence jest as fur as he can on the side of right, and justice to all the citizens of the U.S., wimmen as well as men.

'Tennyrate, he has showed more heroism now than many soldiers who risk life on the battle field. For the worst foe to fight and conquer is Ridicule; and he and others in high places have attackted Fashion so entrenched in the solid armour of Habit that most public men wouldn't have dasted to take arms agin it.

And the long waves of Time must swash up agin the shores of Eternity, before the good it has done can be estimated. How fur the influence has extended. How many weak wills been strengthened. How many broken hearts healed. How many young lives inspired to nobler and saner living.

But to resoom forward, I can't nor won't carry them errents of Serepta's there again. It is too wearin' for one of my age and my rheumatiz. What a tedious time I did put in there. It wuz a day long to be remembered by me.

IX

THE WOMEN'S PARADE

Josiah come home from Jonesville one day, all wrought up. He'd took off a big crate of eggs and got returns from several crates he'd sent to New York, an' he sez to me:

"That consarned Middleman is cheatin' me the worst kind. I know the yaller

Plymouth Rock eggs ort to bring mor'n the white Leghorns; they're bigger

and it stands to reason they're worth more, and he don't give nigh so much.

I believe he eats 'em himself and that's why he wants to git 'em cheaper."

"No Middleman," sez I, "could eat fifty dozen a week."

"He could if he eat enough at one time. 'Tennyrate, I'm goin' to New York to see about it."

"When are you goin'?" sez I.

"I'm goin' to-morrow mornin'. I'm goin' in onexpected and I lay out to catch him devourin' them big eggs himself."

"Oh, shaw!" sez I. "The idee!"

"Well, I say the Trusts and Middlemen are dishonest as the old Harry. Don't you remember what one on 'em writ to Uncle Sime Bentley and what he writ back? He'd sent a great load of potatoes to him and he didn't get hardly anything for 'em, only their big bill for sellin' 'em. They charged him for freightage, carage, storage, porterage, weightage, and to make their bill longer, they put in ratage and satage.

"Uncle Sime writ back 'You infarnel thief, you, put in "stealage" and keep the whole on't.'"

But I sez, "They're not all dishonest. There are good men among 'em as well as bad."

"Well, I lay out to see to it myself, and if they ever charge me for 'ratage' and 'satage' I'm goin' to see what they are, and how they look."

"Well," sez I, "if you're bound to go, I'll get up and get a good breakfast and go with you." It was the day of the Woman's Suffrage Parade and I wanted to see it. I wanted to like a dog, and had ever since I hearn of it. Though some of the Jonesvillians felt different. The Creation Searchin' Society wuz dretful exercised about it. The President's stepma is a strong She Aunty and has always ruled Philander with an iron hand. I've always noticed that women who didn't want any rights always took the right to have their own way. But 'tennyrate Philander come up a very strong He Aunty. And he felt that the Creation Searchers ort to go to New York that day to assist the Aunties in sneerin' at the marchers, writin' up the parade, and helpin' count 'em. Philander wuz always good at figures, specially at subtraction, and he and his Step Ma thought he ort to be there to help.

I told Josiah I guessed the She Aunties didn't need no help at that.

But Philander called a meetin' of the Creation Searchers to make arrangements to go. And I spoze the speech he made at the meetin' wuz a powerful effort. And the members most all on 'em believin' as he did — they said it wuz a dretful interestin' meetin'. Sunthin' like a love feast, only more wrought up and excitin'.

The editor of the Auger printed the whole thing in his paper, and said it give a staggerin' blow agin Woman's Suffrage, and he didn't know but it wuz a death blow — he hoped it wuz.

"A Woman's Parade," sez Philander, "is the most abominable sight ever seen on our planetary system. Onprotected woman dressed up in fine clothes standin' up on her feet, and paradin' herself before strange men. Oh! how bold! Oh! how onwomanly! No wonder," says he, "the She Aunties are shocked at the sight, and say they marched to attract the attention of men. Why can't women stay to home and set down and knit? And then men would love 'em. But if they keep on with these bold, forward actions, men won't love 'em, and they will find out so. And it has always been, and is now, man's greatest desire and chiefest aim he has aimed at, to protect women, to throw the shinin' mantilly of his constant devotion about her delikit form and shield her and guard her like the very apples in his eyes.

"Woman is too sweet and tender a flower to have any such hardship put upon her, and it almost crazes a man, and makes him temporarily out of his head, to see women do anything to hazard that inheriant delicacy of hern, that always appealed so to the male man.

"Let us go forth, clad in our principles (and ordinary clothing, of course), and show just where we stand on the woman question, and do all we can to assist the gentle feminine She Aunties. Lovely, retirin' females whose pictures we so often see gracin' the sensational newspapers. Their white womanly neck and shoulders, glitterin' with jewels, no brighter than their eyes. They don't appear there for sex appeal, or to win admiration. No indeed! No doubt they shrink from the publicity. And also shrink from making speeches in the Senate chambers or the halls of Justice, but will do so, angelic martyrs that they are, to hold their erring Suffrage sisters back from their brazen efforts at publicity and public speakin'."

They said his speech wuz cheered wildly, give out for publication, and entered into the moments of the Society.

But after all, it happened real curious the day of the Parade every leadin' Creation Searcher had some impediment in his way, and couldn't go, and of course, the Society didn't want to go without its leaders.

Mis' Philander Daggett, the president's wife, wuz paperin' her settin' room and parlor overhead. She wuz expectin' company and couldn't put it off. And bein' jest married, and thinkin' the world of her, Philander said he dassent leave home for fear she'd fall offen the barrel and break her neck. She had a board laid acrost two barrels to stand up on. And every day Philander would leave his outside work and come into the house, and set round and watch her—he thought so much of her. I suppose he wanted to catch her if she fell. But I didn't think she would fall. She is young and tuff, and she papered it real good, though it wuz dretful hard on her arm sockets and back.

And the Secretary's wife wuz puttin' in a piece of onions. She thought she would make considerable by it, and she will, if onions keep up. But it is turrible hard on a woman's back to weed 'em. But she is ambitious; she raised a flock of fifty-six turkeys last year besides doin' her house work, and makin' seventy-five yards of rag carpet. And she thought onions wouldn't be so wearin' on her as turkeys, for onions, she said, will stay where they are put, but turkeys are born wanderers and hikers. And they led her through sun and rain, swamp and swale, uphill and downhill, a-chasin' 'em up, but she made well by 'em. Well, in puttin' in her onion seed, she overworked herself and got a crick in her back, so she couldn't stir hand nor foot for two days. And bein' only just them two, her husband had to stay home to see to things.

And the Treasurer's wife is canvassin' for the life of William J. Bryan. And wantin' to make all she could, she took a longer tramp than common, and didn't hear of the Parade or meetin' of the C.S.S. at all. She writ home a day or two before the meetin', that she wuz goin' as long as her legs held out, and they needn't write to her, for she didn't know where she would be.

Well, of course, the Creation Searchers didn't want to go without their officers. They said they couldn't make no show if they did. So they give up goin'. But I spoze they made fun of the Woman's Parade amongst theirselves, and mourned over their indelikit onwomanly actions, and worried about it bein' too hard for 'em, and sneered at 'em considerable.

Well, Josiah always loves to have me with him, an' though he'd made light of the Parade, he didn't object to my goin'. And suffice it to say that we arrove at that Middleman's safe and sound, though why we didn't git lost in that grand immense depo and wander 'round there all day like babes in the woods, is more'n I can tell.

The Middleman wuzn't dishonest: he convinced Josiah on it. He had shipped the colored eggs somewhere, and of course he couldn't pay as much, and he never had hearn of Ratage orSatage. He wuz a real pleasant Middleman, and hearing me say how much I wanted to see the Woman's Parade, he invited us to go upstairs and set by a winder, where there was a good view on't. We'd eat our lunch on the train and we accepted his invitation, and sot down by a winder then and there, though it wuz a hour or so before the time sot for the Parade. And I should have taken solid comfort watchin' the endless procession of men and women and vehicles of all sorts and descriptions, but Josiah made so many slightin' remarks on the dress of the females passin' below on the sidewalk, that it made me feel bad. And to tell the truth, though I didn't think best to own up to it to him, I did blush for my sect to see the way some on 'em rigged themselves out.

"See that thing!" Josiah sez, as a woman passed by with her hat drawed down over one eye, and a long quill standin' out straight behind more'n a foot, an' her dress puckered in so 'round the bottom, she couldn't have took a long step if a mad dog wuz chasin' her—to say nothin' of bein' perched up on such high heels, that she fairly tottled when she walked.

Sez Josiah: "Does that thing know enough to vote?"

"No," sez I, reasonably, "she don't. But most probable if she had bigger things to think about she'd loosen the puckerin' strings 'round her ankles, push her hat back out of her eyes, an' get down on her feet again."

"Why, Samantha," says he, "if you had on one of them skirts tied 'round your ankles, if I wuz a-dyin' on the upper shelf in the buttery, you couldn't step up on a chair to get to me to save your life, an' I'd have to die there alone."

"Why should you be dyin' on the buttery shelf, Josiah?" sez I.

"Oh, that wuz jest a figger of speech, Samantha."

"But folks ort to be mejum in figgers of speech, Josiah, and not go too fur."

"Do you think, Samantha, that anybody can go too fur in describin' them fool skirts, and them slit skirts, and the immodesty and indecensy of some of them dresses?"

"I don't know as they can," sez I, sadly.

"Jest look at that thing," sez he again.

And as I looked, the hot blush of shame mantillied my cheeks, for I felt that my sect was disgraced by the sight. She wuz real pretty, but she didn't have much of any clothes on, and what she did wear wuzn't in the right place; not at all.

Sez Josiah, "That girl would look much more modest and decent if she wuz naked, for then she might be took for a statute."

And I sez, "I don't blame the good Priest for sendin' them away from the Lord's table, sayin', 'I will give no communion to a Jezabel.' And the pity of it is," sez I, "lots of them girls are innocent and don't realize what construction will be put on the dress they blindly copy from some furrin fashion plate."

Then quite an old woman passed by, also robed or disrobed in the prevailin' fashion, and Josiah sez, soty vosy, "I should think she wuz old enough to know sunthin'. Who wants to see her old bones?" And he sez to me, real uppish, "Do you think them things know enough to vote?"

But jest then a young man went by dressed fashionably, but if he hadn't had the arm of a companion, he couldn't have walked a step; his face wuz red and swollen, and dissipated, and what expression wuz left in his face wuz a fool expression, and both had cigarettes in their mouths, and I sez, "Does that thing know enough to vote?" And jest behind them come a lot of furrin laborers, rough and rowdy-lookin', with no more expression in their faces than a mule or any other animal. "Do they know enough to vote?" sez I. "As for the fitness for votin' it is pretty even on both sides. Good intelligent men ortn't to lose the right of suffrage for the vice and ignorance of some of their sect, and that argument is jest as strong for the other sect."

But before Josiah could reply, we hearn the sound of gay music, and the Parade began to march on before us. First a beautiful stately figure seated fearlessly on a dancin' horse, that tossted his head as if proud of the burden he wuz carryin'. She managed the prancin' steed with one hand, and with the other held aloft the flag of our country. Jest as women ort to, and have to. They have got to manage wayward pardners, children and domestics who, no matter how good they are, will take their bits in their mouths, and go sideways some of the time, but can be managed by a sensible, affectionate hand, and with her other hand at the same time she can carry her principles aloft, wavin' in every domestic breeze, frigid or torrid, plain to be seen by everybody.

Then come the wives and relations of Senators and Congressmen, showin' that bein' right on the spot they knowed what wimmen needed. Then the wimmen voters from free Suffrage states, showin' by their noble looks that votin' hadn't hurt 'em any. They carried the most gorgeous banner in the whole Parade. Then the Wimmen's Political Union, showin' plain in their faces that understandin' the laws that govern her ain't goin' to keep woman from looking beautiful and attractive.

On and on they come, gray-headed women and curly-headed children from every station in life: the millionairess by the working woman, and the fashionable society woman by the business one. Two women on horseback, and one blowin' a bugle, led the way for the carriage of Madam Antoinette Blackwell. I wonder if she ever dreamed when she wuz tryin' to climb the hill of knowledge through the thorny path of sex persecution, that she would ever have a bugle blowed in front of her, to honor her for her efforts, and form a part of such a glorious Parade of the sect she give her youth and strength to free.

How they swept on, borne by the waves of music, heralded by wavin' banners of purple and white and gold, bearin' upliftin' and noble mottoes. Physicians, lawyers, nurses, authors, journalists, artists, social workers, dressmakers, milliners, women from furrin countries dressed in their quaint costumes, laundresses, clerks, shop girls, college girls, all bearin' the pennants and banners of their different colleges: Vassar, Wellesley, Smith, etc., etc. High-school pupils, Woman's Suffrage League, Woman's Social League, and all along the brilliant line each division dressed in beautiful costumes and carryin' their own gorgeous banners. And anon or oftener all along the long, long procession bands of music pealin' out high and sweet, as if the Spirit of Music, who is always depictered as a woman, was glad and proud to do honor to her own sect. And all through the Parade you could see every little while men on foot and on horseback, not a great many, but jest enough to show that the really noble men wuz on their side. For, as I've said more formally, that is one of the most convincin' arguments for Woman's Suffrage. In fact, it don't need any other. That bad men fight against Women's Suffrage with all their might.

Down by the big marble library, the grand-stand wuz filled with men seated to see their wives march by on their road to Victory. I hearn and believe, they wuz a noble-lookin' set of men. They had seen their wives in the past chasin' Fashion and Amusement, and why shouldn't they enjoy seein' them follow Principle and Justice? Well, I might talk all day and not begin to tell of the beauty and splendor of the Woman's Parade. And the most impressive sight to me wuz to see how the leaven of individual right and justice had entered into all these different classes of society, and how their enthusiasm and earnestness must affect every beholder.

And in my mind I drawed pictures of the different modes of our American women and our English sisters, each workin' for the same cause, but in what a different manner. Of course, our English sisters may have more reason for their militant doin's; more unjust laws regarding marriage—divorce, and care of children, and I can't blame them married females for wantin' to control their own money, specially if they earnt it by scrubbin' floors and washin'. I can't blame 'em for not wantin' their husbands to take that money from them and their children, specially if they're loafers and drunkards. And, of course, there are no men so noble and generous as our American men. But jest lookin' at the matter from the outside and comparin' the two, I wuz proud indeed of our Suffragists.

While our English sisters feel it their duty to rip and tear, burn and pillage, to draw attention to their cause, and reach the gole (which I believe they have sot back for years) through the smoke and fire of carnage, our American Suffragettes employ the gentle, convincin' arts of beauty and reason. Some as the quiet golden sunshine draws out the flowers and fruit from the cold bosom of the earth. Mindin' their own business, antagonizin' and troublin' no one, they march along and show to every beholder jest how earnest they be. They quietly and efficiently answer that argument of the She Auntys, that women don't want to vote, by a parade two hours in length, of twenty thousand. They answer the argument that the ballot would render women careless in dress and reckless, by organizin' and carryin' on a parade so beautiful, so harmonious in color and design that it drew out enthusiastic praise from even the enemies of Suffrage. They quietly and without argument answered the old story that women was onbusiness-like and never on time, by startin' the Parade the very minute it was announced, which you can't always say of men's parades.

It wuz a burnin' hot day, and many who'd always argued that women hadn't strength enough to lift a paper ballot, had prophesied that woman wuz too delicately organized, too "fraguile," as Betsy Bobbet would say, to endure the strain of the long march in the torrid atmosphere.

But I told Josiah that women had walked daily over the burning plow shares of duty and domestic tribulation, till their feet had got calloused, and could stand more'n you'd think for.

And he said he didn't know as females had any more burnin' plow shares to tread on than men had.

And I sez, "I didn't say they had, Josiah. I never wanted women to get more praise or justice than men. I simply want 'em to get as much—just an even amount; for," sez I, solemnly, "'male and female created He them.'"

Josiah is a deacon, and when I quote Scripture, he has to listen respectful, and I went on: "I guess it wuz a surprise even to the marchers that of all the ambulances that kept alongside the Parade to pick up faint and swoonin' females, the only one occupied wuz by a man."

Josiah denied it, but I sez, "I see his boots stickin' out of the ambulance myself." Josiah couldn't dispute that, for he knows I am truthful. But he sez, sunthin' in the sperit of two little children I hearn disputin'. Sez one: "It wuzn't so; you've told a lie."

"Well," sez the other, "You broke a piece of china and laid it to me."

Sez Josiah, "You may have seen a pair of men's boots a-stickin' out of the ambulance, but I'll bet they didn't have heels on 'em a inch broad, and five or six inches high."

"No, Josiah," sez I, "you're right. Men think too much of their comfort and health to hist themselves up on such little high tottlin' things, and you didn't see many on 'em in the Parade."

But he went on drivin' the arrow of higher criticism still deeper into my onwillin' breast. "I'll bet you didn't see his legs tied together at the ankles, or his trouses slit up the sides to show gauze stockin's and anklets and diamond buckles. And you didn't see my sect who honored the Parade by marchin' in it, have a goose quill half a yard long, standin' up straight in the air from a coal-scuttle hat, or out sideways, a hejus sight, and threatenin' the eyes of friend and foe."

"And you didn't see many on 'em in the Parade," sez I agin. "Women, as they march along to Victory, have got to drop some of these senseless things. In fact, they are droppin' em. You don't see waists now the size of a hour glass. It is gettin' fashionable to breathe now, and women on their way to their gole will drop by the way their high heels; it will git fashionable to walk comfortable, and as they've got to take some pretty long steps to reach the ballot in 1916, it stands to reason they've got to have a skirt wide enough at the bottom to step up on the gole of Victory. It is a high step, Josiah, but women are goin' to take it. They've always tended to cleanin' their own house, and makin' it comfortable and hygenic for its members, big and little. And when they turn their minds onto the best way to clean the National house both sects have to live in to make it clean and comfortable and safe for the weak and helpless as well as for the strong—it stands to reason they won't have time or inclination to stand up on stilts with tied-in ankles, quilled out like savages."

"Well," said Josiah, with a dark, forebodin' look on his linement, "we shall see."

"Yes," sez I, with a real radiant look into the future. "We shall see, Josiah."

But he didn't have no idea of the beautiful prophetic vision I beheld with the eyes of my sperit. Good men and good women, each fillin' their different spears in life, but banded together for the overthrow of evil, the uplift of the race.

X

"THE CREATION SEARCHIN' SOCIETY"

It was only a few days after we got home from New York that Josiah come into the house dretful excited. He'd had a invitation to attend a meetin' of the Creation Searchin' Society.

"Why," sez I, "did they invite you? You are not a member?"

"No," sez he, "but they want me to help 'em be indignant. It is a indignation meetin'."

"Indignant about what?" I sez.

"Fur be it from me, Samantha, to muddle up your head and hurt your feelin's by tellin' you what it's fur." And he went out quick and shet the door. But I got a splendid dinner and afterwards he told me of his own accord.

I am not a member, of course, for the president, Philander Daggett, said it would lower the prestige of the society in the eyes of the world to have even one female member. This meetin' wuz called last week for the purpose of bein' indignant over the militant doin's of the English Suffragettes. Josiah and several others in Jonesville wuz invited to be present at this meetin' as sort of honorary members, as they wuz competent to be jest as indignant as any other male men over the tribulations of their sect.

Josiah said so much about the meetin', and his Honorary Indignation, that he got me curious, and wantin' to go myself, to see how it wuz carried on. But I didn't have no hopes on't till Philander Daggett's new young wife come to visit me and I told her how much I wanted to go, and she bein' real good-natered said she would make Philander let me in.

He objected, of course, but she is pretty and young, and his nater bein' kinder softened and sweetened by the honey of the honeymoon, she got round him. And he said that if we would set up in a corner of the gallery behind the melodeon, and keep our veils on, he would let her and me in. But we must keep it secret as the grave, for he would lose all the influence he had with the other members and be turned out of the Presidential chair if it wuz knowed that he had lifted wimmen up to such a hite, and gin 'em such a opportunity to feel as if they wuz equal to men.

Well, we went early and Josiah left me to Philander's and went on to do some errents. He thought I wuz to spend the evenin' with her in becomin' seclusion, a-knittin' on his blue and white socks, as a woman should. But after visitin' a spell, jest after it got duskish, we went out the back door and went cross lots, and got there ensconced in the dark corner without anybody seein' us and before the meetin' begun.

Philander opened the meetin' by readin' the moments of the last meetin', which wuz one of sympathy with the police of Washington for their noble efforts to break up the Woman's Parade, and after their almost Herculaneum labor to teach wimmen her proper place, and all the help they got from the hoodlum and slum elements, they had failed in a measure, and the wimmen, though stunned, insulted, spit on, struck, broken boneded, maimed, and tore to pieces, had succeeded in their disgustin' onwomanly undertakin'.

But it wuz motioned and carried that a vote of thanks be sent 'em and recorded in the moments that the Creation Searchers had no blame but only sympathy and admiration for the hard worked Policemen for they had done all they could to protect wimmen's delicacy and retirin' modesty, and put her in her place, and no man in Washington or Jonesville could do more. He read these moments, in a real tender sympathizin' voice, and I spoze the members sympathized with him, or I judged so from their linements as I went forward, still as a mouse, and peeked down on 'em.

He then stopped a minute and took a drink of water; I spoze his sympathetic emotions had het him up, and kinder dried his mouth, some. And then he went on to state that this meetin' wuz called to show to the world, abroad and nigh by, the burnin' indignation this body felt, as a society, at the turrible sufferin's and insults bein' heaped onto their male brethren in England by the indecent and disgraceful doin's of the militant Suffragettes, and to devise, if possible, some way to help their male brethren acrost the sea. "For," sez he, "pizen will spread. How do we know how soon them very wimmen who had to be spit on and struck and tore to pieces in Washington to try to make 'em keep their place, the sacred and tender place they have always held enthroned as angels in a man's heart —"

Here he stopped and took out his bandanna handkerchief, and wiped his eyes, and kinder choked. But I knew it wuz all a orator's art, and it didn't affect me, though I see a number of the members wipe their eyes, for this talk appealed to the inheriant chivalry of men, and their desire to protect wimmen, we have always hearn so much about.

"How do we know," he continued, "how soon they may turn aginst their best friends, them who actuated by the loftiest and tenderest emotions, and determination to protect the weaker sect at any cost, took their valuable time to try to keep wimmen down where they ort to be, angels of the home, who knows but they may turn and throw stuns at the Capitol an' badger an' torment our noble lawmakers, a-tryin' to make 'em listen to their silly petitions for justice?"

In conclusion, he entreated 'em to remember that the eye of the world wuz on 'em, expectin' 'em to be loyal to the badgered and woman endangered sect abroad, and try to suggest some way to stop them woman's disgraceful doin's.

Cyrenus Presly always loves to talk, and he always looks on the dark side of things, and he riz up and said "he didn't believe nothin' could be done, for by all he'd read about 'em, the men had tried everything possible to keep wimmen down where they ort to be, they had turned deaf ears to their complaints, wouldn't hear one word they said, they had tried drivin' and draggin' and insults of all kinds, and breakin' their bones, and imprisonment, and stuffin' 'em with rubber tubes, thrust through their nose down into their throats. And he couldn't think of a thing more that could be done by men, and keep the position men always had held as wimmen's gardeens and protectors, and he said he thought men might jest as well keep still and let 'em go on and bring the world to ruin, for that was what they wuz bound to do, and they couldn't be stopped unless they wuz killed off."

Phileman Huffstater is a old bachelder, and hates wimmen. He had been on a drunk and looked dretful, tobacco juice runnin' down his face, his red hair all towsled up, and his clothes stiff with dirt. He wuzn't invited, but had come of his own accord. He had to hang onto the seat in front of him as he riz up and said:

"He believed that wuz the best and only way out on't, for men to rise up and kill off the weaker sect, for their wuzn't never no trouble of any name or nater, but what wimmen wuz to the bottom on't, and the world would be better off without 'em." But Philander scorfed at him and reminded him that such hullsale doin's would put an end to the world's bein' populated at all.

But Phileman said in a hicuppin', maudlin way that "the world had better stop, if there had got to be such doin's, wimmen risin' up on every side, and pretendin' to be equal with men."

Here his knee jints kinder gin out under him, and he slid down onto the seat and went to sleep.

I guess the members wuz kinder shamed of Phileman, for Lime Peedick jumped up quick as scat and said, "It seemed the Englishmen had tried most everything else, and he wondered how it would work if them militant wimmen could be ketched and a dose of sunthin' bitter and sickenin' poured down 'em. Every time they broached that loathsome doctrine of equal rights, and tried to make lawmakers listen to their petitions, jest ketch 'em and pour down 'em a big dose of wormwood or sunthin' else bitter and sickenin', and he guessed they would git tired on't."

But here Josiah jumped up quick and said, "he objected," he said, "that would endanger the right wimmen always had, and ort to have of cookin' good vittles for men and doin' their housework, and bearin' and bringin' up their children, and makin' and mendin' and waitin' on 'em. He said nothin' short of a Gatlin gun could keep Samantha from speakin' her mind about such things, and he wuzn't willin' to have her made sick to the stomach, and incapacitated from cookin' by any such proceedin's."

The members argued quite awhile on this pint, but finally come round to Josiah's idees, and the meetin' for a few minutes seemed to come to a standstill, till old Cornelius Snyder got up slowly and feebly. He has spazzums and can't hardly wobble. His wife has to support him, wash and dress him, and take care on him like a baby. But he has the use of his tongue, and he got some man to bring him there, and he leaned heavy on his cane, and kinder stiddied himself on it and offered this suggestion:

"How would it do to tie females up when they got to thinkin' they wuz equal to men, halter 'em, rope 'em, and let 'em see if they wuz?"

But this idee wuz objected to for the same reason Josiah had advanced, as Philander well said, "wimmen had got to go foot loose in order to do the housework and cookin'."

Uncle Sime Bentley, who wuz awful indignant, said, "I motion that men shall take away all the rights that wimmen have now, turn 'em out of the meetin' house, and grange."

But before he'd hardly got the words out of his mouth, seven of the members riz up and as many as five spoke out to once with different exclamations:

"That won't do! we can't do that! Who'll do all the work! Who'll git up grange banquets and rummage sales, and paper and paint and put down carpets in the meetin' house, and git up socials and entertainments to help pay the minister's salary, and carry on the Sunday School? and tend to its picnics and suppers, and take care of the children? We can't do this, much as we'd love to."

One horsey, sporty member, also under the influence of liquor, riz up, and made a feeble motion, "Spozin' we give wimmen liberty enough to work, leave 'em hand and foot loose, and sort o' muzzle 'em so they can't talk."

This seemed to be very favorably received, 'specially by the married members, and the secretary wuz jest about to record it in the moments as a scheme worth tryin', when old Doctor Nugent got up, and sez in a firm, decided way:

"Wimmen cannot be kept from talking without endangerin' her life; as a medical expert I object to this motion."

"How would you put the objection?" sez the secretary.

"On the ground of cruelty to animals," sez the doctor.

A fat Englishman who had took the widder Shelmadine's farm on shares, says, "I 'old with Brother Josiah Hallen's hargument. As the father of nine young children and thirty cows to milk with my wife's 'elp, I 'old she musn't be kep' from work, but h'I propose if we can't do anything else that a card of sympathy be sent to hold Hengland from the Creation Searchin' Society of America, tellin' 'em 'ow our 'earts bleeds for the men's sufferin' and 'ardships in 'avin' to leave their hoccupations to beat and 'aul round and drive females to jails, and feed 'em with rubber hose through their noses to keep 'em from starvin' to death for what they call their principles."

This motion wuz carried unanimously.

But here an old man, who had jest dropped in and who wuz kinder deef and slow-witted, asked, "What it is about anyway? what do the wimmen ask for when they are pounded and jailed and starved?"

Hank Yerden, whose wife is a Suffragist, and who is mistrusted to have a leanin' that way himself, answered him, "Oh, they wanted the lawmakers to read their petitions asking for the rights of ordinary citizens. They said as long as their property wuz taxed they had the right of representation. And as long as the law punished wimmen equally with men, they had a right to help make that law, and as long as men claimed wimmen's place wuz home, they wanted the right to guard that home. And as long as they brought children into the world they wanted the right to protect 'em. And when the lawmakers wouldn't hear a word they said, and beat 'em and drove 'em round and jailed 'em, they got mad as hens, and are actin' like furiation and wild cats. But claim that civil rights wuz never give to any class without warfare."

"Heavens! what doin's!" sez old Zephaniah Beezum, "what is the world comin' to!" "Angle worms will be risin' up next and demandin' to not be trod on." Sez he, "I have studied the subject on every side, and I claim the best way to deal with them militant females is to banish 'em to some barren wilderness, some foreign desert where they can meditate on their crimes, and not bother men."

This idee wuz received favorably by most of the members, but others differed and showed the weak p'ints in it, and it wuz gin up.

Well, at ten P.M., the Creation Searchers gin up after arguin' pro and con, con and pro, that they could not see any way out of the matter, they could not tell what to do with the wimmen without danger and trouble to the male sect.

They looked dretful dejected and onhappy as they come to this conclusion, my pardner looked as if he wuz most ready to bust out cryin'. And as I looked on his beloved linement I forgot everything else and onbeknown to me I leaned over the railin' and sez:

"Here is sunthin' that no one has seemed to think on at home or abroad. How would it work to stop the trouble by givin' the wimmen the rights they ask for, the rights of any other citizen?"

I don't spoze there will ever be such another commotion and upheaval in Jonesville till Michael blows his last trump as follered my speech. Knowin' wimmen wuz kep' from the meetin', some on 'em thought it wuz a voice from another spear. Them wuz the skairt and horrow struck ones, and them that thought it wuz a earthly woman's voice wuz so mad that they wuz by the side of themselves and carried on fearful. But when they searched the gallery for wimmen or ghosts, nothin' wuz found, for Philander's wife and I had scooted acrost lots and wuz to home a-knittin' before the men got there.

And I d'no as anybody but Philander to this day knows what, or who it wuz.

And I d'no as my idee will be follered, but I believe it is the best way out on't for men and wimmen both, and would stop the mad doin's of the English Suffragettes, which I don't approve of, no indeed! much as I sympathize with the justice of their cause.

Milton Keynes UK
Ingram Content Group UK Ltd.
UKHW050710220124
436466UK00017B/731